MAN IN TROUBLE

Al Riley—ex-astronaut trainee, downed jet pilot, American "spy" in Soviet custody—drew the trembling girl closer in the naked privacy of his prison cell.

Her soft hand stroked his stiff growth of beard. "If I was shaved," he whispered, aware of the listening devices in the wall, "you'd be in trouble."

Judith smiled in her enigmatic Oriental way. "The beard is nice," she said. "Very mannish."

He knew now why she'd been sent to him—and what he had to do—to save her from further brutalization by her Communist masters, and himself from execution as a spy.

AUTHOR'S PROFILE

Tedd Thomey was born in Butte, Montana in 1920 and is a graduate of the University of California. He served in the Marine Corps as a second lieutenant during World War II.

After his war stint he became a reporter and feature writer on the San Diego UNION-TRIBUNE and the San Francisco CHRONICLE and he is currently a columnist and telegraph editor on the Long Beach INDEPENDENT-PRESS-TELEGRAM.

He has been a professional free lance writer for 12 years and is the author of a recent Monarch fiction bestseller entitled WHEN THE LUSTING BEGAN.

A Contemporary Novel

FLIGHT
TO TAKLA-MA

Tedd Thomey

WILDSIDE PRESS

⌒⤜(chapter one)⤛⌒

The throat valve failed again while Riley was immersed in the test tank.

Inside the white astronaut helmet, Riley's dark, high-cheek-boned face instantly grew hot and he began to choke. Holding his breath, he shot to the surface of the water and signaled to the civilian technicians watching him from the edge of the tank.

He did not panic. He knew they would get him out in time and they did. Strong arms hoisted him from the water and quickly removed the five-pound helmet, giving him unlimited quantities of fresh, clean air.

"Second time this week!" Riley said, still gasping. "Where the hell is the commander?"

"In the storeroom," said one of the technicians. "He's—"

"Thanks!" said Riley.

He took the thick, plastic helmet from the technician's hands, turned and walked angrily toward a doorway at the rear of the large Quonset hut. He was a tall man, six feet one and thirty years old, and as he strode along the edge of the test tank, water dripped from the glittering surfaces of his aluminized Mark IV pressure suit, leaving a dark, irregular trail behind him on the concrete floor. In anger his tanned face reflected even more strength than usual, muscle ridging up along his jaw, a dimple going deep into his left cheek, his dark brown eyes flashing fire.

He found Commander Truslow checking astronaut suits which hung in the storeroom like a row of limp corpses.

It did not matter to Riley that Truslow outranked him.

"Goddamn it!" said Riley. "Are you trying to kill me?"

Truslow turned around and looked at him peevishly. He was a small, scientific-appearing naval officer who

5

never seemed at ease in the presence of the tall, muscular men whom he outfitted in layers of rubber, plastic and nylon.

"Of course not," he said. "What's the matter now?"

"Valve stuck again!" said Riley. "I thought you said it was fixed!"

"So it was, Major."

"Then what's wrong with it?"

Riley offered the helmet to Truslow, but the commander did not take it from his hands.

"Could be any number of things."

"Like lousy design, maybe?"

Truslow's face colored. "I doubt that. I designed that valve personally, Major, and I feel certain it's highly workable."

"Highly workable crap!" said Riley. "The damn thing's no good!"

"Now see here, Major. I won't have you—"

"Redesign it," said Riley. "I suggest that you redesign the damn thing completely. It's—"

"You've got your nerve!" Truslow's thin voice rose until it was almost shrill. "I'm very familiar with your record, Major. I happen to know there's not one engineering course in your background—and yet you have the nerve to tell me my valve's no good! I happen to know you were kicked out of UCLA! I happen to know your Air Force record is only so-so and you just barely got into this training program. And yet you have the audacity to—"

"Fix it!" said Riley.

Again he offered the helmet to Truslow and again Truslow refused to take it.

Riley did not hesitate. Raising the white helmet high in the air, he jammed it down hard upon Truslow's head. Truslow tried to dodge, but succeeded only in knocking his khaki overseas cap awry. As the helmet came down firmly in place, its round edge caught the khaki cap. The cap vanished for a moment and then became visible through the helmet's clear plastic visor. It was now wedged crookedly against Truslow's eyes and small pointed nose.

The effect was so ludicrous Riley would have laughed if he hadn't been so angry.

He strode from the storeroom, went into the locker room across the corridor and began to remove his pressure suit. He knew there would be repercussions. There were always repercussions whenever he lost his temper. Inherited from a hot-blooded Irish-American father and a hot-blooded Latin mother, his temper had been a problem during all of his eventful three decades of life.

A head appeared in the locker room doorway.

"You going?" said Jensen, one of the technicians.

"Going where?"

"To the beach party. We're leaving in ten minutes."

Riley took his wrist watch from the locker, saw that it was four-thirty and put it on.

"Count me in," he said. "Where's Truslow?"

"Hightailing it to the Administration Building."

"He would," said Riley.

"What did you do about the helmet?"

"Not enough. I should've rammed it up his butt."

"And then some," said Jensen. "See you in ten minutes."

Riley dressed in freshly laundered Air Force suntans and slanted a blue overseas cap at the correct angle across his dark, crew-cut hair. As he walked from the air-conditioned Quonset into the warm, humid outdoors, the anger was still bitterly heavy within him. He knew he should stop thinking about Truslow and the valve foul-up, but he could not. He looked around for Jensen's station wagon, didn't see it and strode to the tall, red soft-drink machine which stood in the shade of the building's aluminum-roofed breezeway.

The Coke tasted good. It was warmer than usual for February in Florida, nearly ninety even this late in the afternoon, and he had sweated out a lot of body fluid during the immersion test. He looked across the base, saw the silvery heat waves writhing above the curved roofs of a dozen other Quonsets and he had a feeling of pride as he thought about the difficult tests he had successfully concluded within those buildings.

This was Mercury Beach, the most elite and exclusive training center in the world. This was where man gained the knowledge to combat the unknowns of space. He had fought like hell to get here and he wasn't about to let a nervous little character like Truslow spoil his chances. Certainly not now, when his tests were nearly over.

A medium-sized blond man in Navy khaki came along the flagstone path and put a coin in the Coke machine.

"How you doing?" he asked.

"Okay," Riley said.

The man nodded and as he stepped closer Riley recognized him as one of a score of new officers who had arrived at the base two weeks previously. He wore the bars of a senior lieutenant on his collar and Riley didn't need to see the golden wings above his shirt pocket to know he was one of the astronaut candidates. The other signs were all there—the trim waist, the squint lines around the eyes and, most important of all, the strong self-confidence he displayed even in the simple act of tilting back his head to drink thirstily from the green bottle.

"I'm Exler," he said, extending his palm. "Been here long?"

"Couple of months," said Riley. He introduced himself and they shook hands firmly.

"Lucky bastard," said Exler. "Wish I was in your boots. I've still got ten or eleven tests to go." He shook his head thoughtfully. "Heat, cold, decompression, the works. Confidentially, Major, is that ride in the centrifuge as bad as they say it is?"

"Just about."

"How many Gs did you pull?"

"A little over 8.6."

"Jesus!" Drying his mouth on the back of his hand, Exler placed his empty bottle on the metal rack. "Some merry-go-round!"

"And no music," said Riley.

They grinned at one another and then looked out at

8

the street where a horn was being tooted on Jensen's arriving station wagon.

"Big beach party," said Riley. "Want to come?"

"Can't make it," said Exler. "I've got thermal tests tonight and tomorrow."

'Some other time." Riley started walking toward the station wagon and then he looked back at Exler over his shoulder.

"Be sure and double-check your gear," he said. "And watch that new throat valve. It's tricky."

"Will do." Exler gave him a jaunty wave. "Thanks."

During the ride to the strand, Riley bantered with the other men and made the expected comments on what kind of women would be at the party. But half his thoughts dwelled on Commander Truslow. It was unfortunate that Truslow was considered an engineering genius by the brass at Mercury Beach, who were willing to ignore his nervousness and pettiness.

There undoubtedly would be trouble in the morning; Truslow would see to that. All of it would be easily explained except the way he'd jammed the space helmet down over Truslow's head. He never should have lost his temper. And he would have to be careful not to lose it again in the morning.

It was dusk when Riley and the others piled out of the station wagon at the beach, and the last hot sliver of Florida sun was dissolving into the twilight gray waters of the Atlantic.

The party was already well under way, with about a dozen people gathered in small groups. Some of the girls were playing volleyball, the men who had arrived early were drinking beer from cans, and a small fire of cypress branches was casting fragrant embers into the moist, breezeless air.

"Where do we change?" asked Riley.

"Over there," shouted one of the girls, pointing to a cluster of small palm trees. "We're informal tonight."

The men laughed and Riley went with the others behind the inadequate palm fronds and began removing his suntans.

9

"Hey," whispered Jensen, "who's that?"

She stood at the edge of the volleyball group, but for the moment she was not playing. She was a blonde, a leggy, pure-bred blonde, and she stood there gazing boldly at the undressing men.

"First name's Fay," whispered someone else. "One of the new gals."

"Last name's Exler," said another. "A sizzler."

"Goddamn it, Riley," said Jensen, "you have all the luck. It's you she's looking at."

It was true. At first Riley hadn't thought so, but she stood close enough so it was possible to determine that her eyes had singled him out. He was not embarrassed. He turned his naked body only slightly away from her gaze and donned a pair of brown trunks which closely matched the reddish-brown tan of his skin.

She remained there a moment more, looking at him, and as she turned and rejoined the volleyball game he realized where he had heard her name before. Exler. The Navy lieutenant he'd met at the Coke machine.

"It's your serve, Fay," one of the women called.

She nodded and moved gracefully away from the net. He noticed that several of the other women in the group were pretty, even beautiful, but with Fay Exler in their midst they might as well have been painted figures cut from plywood.

She wore a strapless bathing suit of a white rubberized material which fitted so smoothly it was a second skin. It revealed nothing and yet it revealed everything. When she leaped from the white sand to strike the ball, her long yellow hair moved beautifully and her breasts, large but perfectly formed, rose and fell with a movement that stopped every male eye in the crowd.

Riley didn't wait for a pause in the game. He took two cans of beer from the picnic table, walked up to her and offered her one.

"Hello," he said. "I'm Al Riley."

"Thank you," she said, accepting the beer. "Care to join the game?"

"Later, maybe. Right now I'd like to go for a walk."

10

He took her elbow and tried to steer her toward the darkening surf, but she slipped away from him and walked toward the fire.

"I'm getting hungry," she said. "How about some franks?"

"Sounds swell."

They took frankfurters and long-handled wire forks from the picnic table and knelt before the fire. And now that he was close enough to smell her light perfume he could appreciate more fully how young she was and how clear her complexion was.

She was at most twenty-two or twenty-three. She was tall, but she had none of the heaviness often seen in large girls. Her hips were slimly curved and her legs, folded modestly against the sand, displayed a beautiful, slender firmness.

As he reached out, holding his fork over the flame, his shoulder touched hers. She did not draw away. Her skin was warm against his and for a moment her blue eyes looked at him with the same boldness as before, when he was undressing, and he felt the blood begin to beat more strongly in his throat. She impaled a plump frank on her fork, extended it into the gray curling smoke and her shoulder moved away from his.

"Do you know my name?" she asked.

"Yes."

"I wish you didn't."

"Why?" He looked at her with surprise.

"Because I want us to be strangers."

She said it quietly, but with conviction, and it was hard to tell by her tone exactly what she meant. For some reason her mood had become pensive and downcast.

Before he could ask her a clarifying question, another couple joined them at the fire and began roasting franks. Soon they were joined by still others and their conversation was limited to impersonal comments on the food and the smoke which occasionally drifted into their eyes.

But as the sky darkened and more beer was consumed, the party grew emphatically more gay. An Air Force technician plugged an electric guitar into the battery on

11

his Ford hardtop and began strumming dance tunes with a surprisingly good beat. It was exactly what the crowd wanted.

Everybody danced, including Riley and Fay, and no one objected to the fact that the deep, uneven sand interfered with their steps, making it necessary for the couples to cling tightly and move somewhat slower than the music suggested. There was lots of laughing and lots of casual kissing.

Fay did not seem to mind when Riley held her very close and danced her into the darkness away from the fire. Her mood was far different now, animated and sparkling.

When he tried to kiss her, she dodged playfully, laughing at him. Then she caught his head between her palms and kissed him accurately, full on the lips. And just as quickly she drew away, laughing again.

"Well, how do you do?" he said softly. He returned her kiss, holding her tightly, finding her mouth delightfully fresh and warm.

"Fine," she said, slightly out of breath. "And you?"

"Very fine."

The words themselves didn't matter at all. What did matter was the very personal way they were spoken and the hidden meaning behind them.

"How about that walk now?" he queried.

"Not yet." She saw the disappointment in his eyes and smiled up at him, her eyes warmly reflecting the firelight. "This *is* a beach party, isn't it? Don't you think we should go for a swim?"

"Sold."

Seizing her hand, he pulled her running across the sand and they plunged into the calm dark surf. The water was invigorating, neither warm nor cool, and they shouted together and kicked up a high spray.

Still holding her hand, he drew her farther out, until the water was nearly to her shoulders and then he pulled her close and kissed her, more firmly than before. She did not pull away when he touched her breasts lightly beneath the water. Instead she pressed herself against him and he realized that her excitement was beginning to equal his own.

"Shall we go walking now?" he asked.

"Yes," she said and he sensed her eagerness. "Oh, yes."

As they left the water, he noticed there were fewer couples dancing now, many of the others having moved their private necking parties into the shadows of the palm trees.

He and Fay walked along the water's edge, finding the sand as hard-packed and smooth as macadam. They walked for many minutes until the fire was a match-sized flame in the blackness behind them and then Riley led her behind a sloping dune which provided a semi-circle of shelter.

They sat down close together and looked out at the surf. She was more quiet now and he wondered if her earlier mood had returned.

"What did you mean back there?" he said. "Back at the fire, before supper, when you said you wanted us to be strangers?"

"I meant it," she said.

"But you seemed troubled."

"Troubled?" She hesitated. "Perhaps. But I meant what I said. I like to do exactly what we're doing. I like to sit on the beach like this with a stranger. And you will remain a stranger, won't you?"

"It depends. Do you really want me to?"

"Yes. I want you to remain a stranger and to keep that look I saw in your eyes when you were taking your shirt off behind the palms."

"What look?"

"That all-man look. As if you'd like to devour me in one big bite."

They laughed together, easily, and she tipped her head back and looked up at the stars. He bent over her and as he kissed her she moved quickly against him and clasped her hands around his neck. Then, their lips still together, she let her weight pull him down gradually to the sand. He felt the mounds of her breasts beneath his chest, felt the growing heat of her mouth and felt the blood beating fiercely in his throat and in the pit of his abdomen.

Their lips separated for a moment but they did not speak or whisper. She pressed her large strong body harder against his and they kissed again, with deeper, more demanding contact. Her breasts moved against him like nothing he had ever felt before.

He kissed her cheek, her throat, her shoulder and then with a quick motion he drew her strapless bathing suit part way down until one of her large breasts was revealed. He kissed its tip, the nipple hard and thrusting, and felt her draw her breath in sharply.

She cried out and the thought that he could have her now, this instant, filled him with animal power. Both his hands seized the top of her suit and pulled it downward, but then her hands caught his and restrained him.

"I want to!" she cried "Believe me, I want you, too!"

"Then why not?"

"Not tonight. Not with the others so near."

"Damn you!" he said.

"Tomorrow night, I promise!"

His voice rose with anger. "Damn you! I ought to—"

But she was wise in the arts of love. Because she knew she was in danger of being assaulted, she cooled his ardor with less intimate kisses, and returned her bathing suit to a position of safety. Gradually she withdrew from him and then she stood and brushed the white sand from her long yellow hair.

"I know you hate me," she said.

He did not comment. He was dangerously close to losing his temper. To prevent another incident like the one with Commander Truslow, he closed his hands and dropped them to his sides.

"Don't be cross," she said. "Tomorrow night, I promise."

"You're lying," he retorted.

She ignored the cut in his voice. "I want it to be here." She gestured at the protective dune. "And I want you to be a stranger again."

During the walk back to the party, they did not speak.

14

But before they joined the others, she gave him a provocative smile that made him think she was telling the truth after all.

"Meet me at Italio's," she said. "At six. And bring some sparkling Burgundy."

chapter two

The next day, Wednesday, was a long one, full of more frustrations. The helmet's throat valve was still defective and Commander Truslow absented himself from the training center early in the morning, obviously to delay contact with Riley until he was good and ready. None of the technicians could make the valve function properly.

Riley left Mercury Beach late in the afternoon and drove his yellow convertible into the nearby town of Kellton. He didn't really expect to find her at Italio's. But she came—exactly at six.

They met in the restaurant's smart, Neapolitan cocktail lounge and he was struck again by the physical magnificence of her. She wore white once more, a simple off-the-shoulder frock which beautifully emphasized her Nordic coloring and the pure blondness of her long hair.

"Hi," he said. "Thirsty?"

"Definitely." She smiled so warmly he knew at once that tonight would be far different from last night.

They had superb Martinis, two each, and then they went into one of the small, quiet dining rooms and began a leisurely dinner of antipasto, minestrone and beef ravioli. He had no desire to rush her. They talked of many impersonal things, cities they'd visited and enjoyed, movies they'd seen and the better shows on television.

It was while they were finishing their spumoni dessert that she brought up the subject of her husband. She

15

did it easily but quite directly, and her blue eyes contained a hint of vindictiveness.

"He has his fun," she said. "I have mine."

"Other women?" Riley asked. "Is that what was troubling you last night?"

"Yes. Partly."

"I'm sorry to hear it."

"Don't be," she said. "It was something else that put the first cracks in our marriage."

"Do you want to talk about it?"

"Not especially. But it's his work, of course. We quarreled and quarreled, but he insisted on applying for Mercury Beach—even though he knew what it would do to me."

She placed her spoon crosswise on her ice cream plate and was silent for a moment.

"He has the duty tonight," she said. "More tests."

"Mine are being delayed," Riley said. "Defective equipment."

"Oh?" She looked at him strangely. "I was afraid of that."

"Afraid of what?"

"Afraid you'd be one of the astronauts. And you are, aren't you?"

He shook his head. "Not quite. I'm one of the candidates, one of dozens of back-up men in the program. I hope to be chosen, if I'm lucky."

Suddenly the color was gone from her cheeks, leaving her face somber and pale around the bright orange-red of her lipstick. When she spoke again, her voice was very subdued.

"You'll be chosen. I know you will. And you'll be killed. I know you'll all be killed."

He laughed at her, trying to reassure her, but her face remained serious and for the first time he realized there was more to her than a woman on the make.

"Why do you do it?" she said. "Why must you fly higher? And then higher." Her fingers seized his arm and held it tightly. "Why must you do it?"

"It's our job."

"That's no answer," she responded bitterly. "Do you say that because there is no real answer?"

"No."

"Then what is it?" she demanded. "What is the real answer?"

For a long moment he was silent, trying to find a way to express something which he had thought about many times but which he had never put into words.

"Because it's a test of a man," he said. "The higher he goes the more a man reveals what he is."

She remained thoughtful a moment. Finally she said, "Yes, that must be partly it. But for a woman, waiting and waiting, it means constant fear. It brings compulsions. And sometimes a woman's only defense is to love her husband less and less."

He interrupted her with chiding laughter. "Hey," he said, "I thought we were supposed to be strangers. We won't be if we keep on like this."

She hesitated, then laughed with him and some of the color returned to her cheeks. "By all means," she said and the gaiety in her voice did not seem forced. "Did you bring the wine, stranger?"

"It's in the car, stranger," he said. "On ice. Shall we go?

During the ride to the beach, she sat close to him, her thigh against his, and they talked of small, unimportant things and made love with their eyes and hands.

It was dark when he parked near the strand and there were no other cars near. They found their private dune almost at once and slipped down onto the sand behind its protective shoulder. They kissed many times, eagerly, and he passed his hands over her body and tugged at the zipper at her side.

"No," she said. "First the wine, lots of wine, and then—"

They had fun when the cork popped and the bubbly red Burgundy foamed from the heavy bottle. They touched glasses, drank and refilled them. The wine flavored their kisses delightfully and when the first bottle was finished they were lighthearted and jubilant.

17

Fay drew her white bathing suit from her large purse, held it up and then cast it aside.

"To hell with it!" she said cheerfully.

She rose to her feet and in a few seconds slipped from her dress, bra and panties. She let him see her beautiful nude body for only a moment, then she turned and ran gracefully into the surf.

He stripped off his clothes and followed her. The water was waist-deep when he captured her, warmish but exhilarating. He drew her very close, feeling her wet breasts, tasting the salt water on his lips, thrusting his leg between hers. He lifted her into his arms and carried her with a rush of water and excitement up onto the beach.

Placing her on the sand, he covered her body with his own. She was remarkable from the beginning, her movements vigorous and unselfish. They forgot everything. There was no fear for them, no uncertain future, no guilt. For them there was only desire and demand compounded a thousand times, and the magnificence of knowing that these moments, no matter what else happened, were as real as God could make them.

Physically they were perfectly matched, and from the moment she caught and joined his propelling rhythm, he knew he had found a woman who regarded this ritual with the same frank, hedonistic delight as he did— a calculated but abandoned pursuit of the ultimate in exquisite awareness. She was with him all the way, from the slow joy-piercing take-off, through the steady breath-taking climb, as they drove higher and higher, plunging toward unimaginable heights of sensation, till, somewhere in outer space, their world blew wide-open in a jet explosion of total ecstasy.

Later they lay together in the darkness behind the dune, their warm legs touching, and slowly drank the second bottle of the wine.

"I feel so good," she said. "For a while I have nothing to be afraid of."

"Only for a while?"

"Yes, because—" She paused, and then her voice be-

18

came cheerful again. "Oh, I feel so very, very good. Let's go swimming, shall we?"

He took her hand and they ran back to the water. He noticed that she was tipsy from the wine and he felt the effects of it also—a buoyant, hollow feeling at the back of his head. He dived in, washing the sand from his face and hair, and swam strongly for several strokes. She swam close beside him, her long yellow hair streaming wetly behind her. Then she called to him, urging him to swim faster. Increasing the speed of her strokes, she drew ahead.

She was not a smooth swimmer but she was powerful and he let her get more than a dozen yards beyond him, before he tried to catch her. He swam under water, feeling very relaxed from the wine. But when he arose with a great splash at the place where he expected her to be she was not there. He swam further, looking for her in the darkness, then turned and swam back.

She was not there either. It occurred to him that she might be teasing and he swam in a large slow circle, expecting her to pop up at any moment, laughing and shouting. But when he saw her it was not like that at all.

She was struggling. She was mostly under water, with just her hands showing, beating at the surface. As soon as he reached her, he knew she had overestimated her swimming ability because of the wine.

He caught her hand and at once she was a wild nude thing of panic, flailing at him, kicking, trying to grasp him. He shook her off and tried to pin her arms behind her back, but her panic gave her enormous strength and she clamped an arm around his neck and bore them both deeply downward. He brook loose and instantly she clamped her muscular legs around his waist.

He knew he had to hit her then. He had to aim by instinct because the water was a dark film against his eyes. He struck her on the side of the face, but the blow stimulated her struggles. Again he struck, harder this time, extremely hard, and immediately she went limp and he was able to bring her to the surface.

19

From that point on everything rushed together too quickly. When he pulled her up to the beach to begin mouth-to-mouth resuscitation, her head was twisted at an unusual angle.

She did not respond. He turned her over and pressed a little water from her lungs, but it did not help.

In vain he tried more mouth-to-mouth breathing and then he placed his ear to her chest. There was a faint heartbeat, almost nonexistent.

Covering her with the white dress, he placed her carefully on the back seat of the convertible. He pulled on his swim trunks and then drove as swiftly as he dared, cutting in and out of traffic on the beach road, running through amber and red lights.

Once, trapped for part of a hellish minute in a throng of unmoving cars, he spoke to her.

"Fay?" He glanced back at her. "Can you hear me, Fay?"

She did not speak. Nor did she move. And fear was a heavy, formless object within him.

He drove her to the emergency entrance of the small community hospital at Kellton.

The doctors took her at once into surgery and left Riley sitting alone in an air-conditioned waiting room which chilled his naked shoulders and made him shiver.

Sooner than expected, the surgeon returned. He was a young man with intelligent gray eyes and he wore a white smock and a gauze mask which hung loosely beneath his chin.

"My God!" said Riley. "Don't look at me like that. Is it her neck? Will she be paralyzed?"

The doctor reached out and touched Riley's arm. "We couldn't operate," he said gently. "She died while we were wheeling her in."

Riley stared at him, trying not to believe the fantastic words, but knowing all the time that they were true.

Then he bowed his head and covered his face with his cold, shaking hands.

～✦(chapter three)✦～

The dream was ended. The dream of flying higher and higher into the midnight blue where no man had gone before him. The dream of flying at speeds no man had reached before. The dream of being one of the first.

Even before the inquest returned its verdict of excusable homicide, Major Alfred Coronado Riley, USAF, knew he was through, washed up, kicked out. After it was over he could have escaped through the side door of the coroner's office and driven away without talking to Fay's husband but he did not.

He waited on the cracked sidewalk in front of the shabby courthouse. And when Lieutenant Exler came down the concrete steps, he offered his hand and tried to express a few of the thoughts that were jammed up within him.

"I know you hate my guts," he began. "And I don't blame you—"

"Bastard," said Exler. "Out of my way!"

He brushed Riley's hand aside as he strode past and gave him a glance of dark fury and hate. He walked on a few steps, then spun on his heel and spoke to Riley again, his words loud enough to be heard by the others leaving the courthouse.

"Son of a bitch," he said. "You lousy rotten son of a bitch!"

Riley did not turn away until Exler had disappeared around the corner of the building. Then he walked to his car and drove back to the base.

There was no hearing in the CO's headquarters, no chance to defend himself, no opportunity to explain how it happened.

The meeting in Truslow's office took less than a minute. Truslow's small, pointed features twitched with nervousness, but his voice was carefully composed.

"Major Riley," he said, "you've bought it. Here are your orders."

He handed over a clean, manila envelope. There's a MATS transport leaving at five. Be on it."

And that was that.

He was transferred to Edwards Air Force Base in the California desert and returned to his old duties test-flying jets. But it was weeks before he could sleep the whole night through.

Fay was on his mind always. He thought about how emotionally mixed up she was, offering herself to him, seeking sensations which could only further confuse her feelings for her husband and her fears for his safety. He did not spare himself from thinking about the blow which had broken her neck. He thought about it a hundred times a day.

The other pilots at Edwards never talked about it. To him, at least. But there was a barrier between him and some of the pilots, mostly the married ones. There was a coldness in their attitude toward him and they developed a noticeable way of breaking up conversations when he approached.

He did not drink more than usual. Instead he tried to lose himself in his flying. If a speed run called for 1,300 miles an hour, he exceeded it because the danger kept him from thinking about other things. If a structural integrity test called for a screaming dive at 8.5 Gs, he exceeded it—for the same reason.

But even in this he failed. They ordered him to stop exceeding the test specifications. And when he persisted they reduced him to further bitterness by assigning him to routine duties in slower airplanes.

And then he met McKnight.

At first McKnight hung back, deliberately making no impression upon him. Standing on the concrete apron one afternoon at the test flight hangar, McKnight appeared to be a member of a visiting group of engineers from Los Angeles.

But that night McKnight showed up at the pilots'

22

BOQ, standing on the fringe of the cocktail crowd, saying very little to anyone. He was conspicuous, however, for several reasons—his extreme height, his extreme thinness, his beautifully tailored sports clothes and his age. He was at least sixty-five, perhaps much older, a decrepit age by the standards of the men at Edwards.

The following morning, McKnight was at the briefings. He was introduced to Riley, they spoke a few words and that seemed to be all of it.

But on the next day Riley received word that he was to report to Building L-3 for an interview.

"What kind of an interview?" he asked Noonan, the administrative officer.

"I don't know," said Noonan. "But that old boy gave me one hell of a top priority to get you over there."

He found McKnight seated alone in the office of the assistant operations officer. It was a plain room with a concrete floor, badly nailed plywood walls, three wooden chairs and a desk which had been in need of varnish for many years.

"Good morning, Major," said McKnight, seated behind the desk. "Before you sit down would you make certain the door is locked?"

Riley snapped the bolt, then placed himself on the wooden chair nearest the desk. He crossed his legs and waited for McKnight to begin the interview.

But McKnight did not speak. He sat very erect in his chair, both palms resting on the desk, and stared at Riley.

Riley stared back, taking note of McKnight's probing gray eyes, his once blond hair which was now a yellowish white and his pale skin which bore many fine wrinkles like high-quality paper that had been crumpled and recrumpled many times.

They stared for ten seconds, twenty, with neither man willing to look away.

Finally when the discomfort was at its peak, McKnight spoke. "Is Riley your real name?"

"Yes."

"Riley is a British name, isn't it? Or is it Irish?"

"Irish."

23

"But you don't have an Irishman's skin. It's darker, almost Latin in color. And your eyes are what I call dark Spanish brown."

"Is there any crime in that?"

"Of course not. You are, therefore, of mixed parentage?"

"Yes."

"Your father was Irish?"

"My father was *not* Irish," said Riley. "He was an American."

"Very good. Your mother?"

"She was Mexican."

"I see. Therefore you have your mother's complexion, more or less, and your father's large bony frame."

"Goddamn it," said Riley angrily, "who gives a damn about my mother's skin and my father's bones! I was born in Los Angeles, U.S.A., and I've lived in this country all my life!"

"Excellent," said McKnight, "but there's—"

"If you don't mind," said Riley, "I'd like to know a few things about you, McKnight. What right do you have to make insinuations about my background? Who do you work for and what's the purpose of this interview?"

McKnight did not reply at once. His eyes shone with a remarkable intensity, but seemingly more from exasperation than anger.

"I work for the United States government," he said.

"What division?"

"You will be told if and when I feel you should know." McKnight's voice grew cold. "I am being very patient with you, Major. Do you wish to continue with the interview?"

"Yes."

"Thank you." McKnight cleared his throat. "I have studied your records, Major, and I have questions to ask. I saw a notation, for example, that you were an outstanding sprinter at UCLA. Is that correct?"

"More or less."

"And yet you were kicked out of UCLA. Why?"

"I didn't spend enough time studying."

"Any other reason?"

"Possibly." Riley shrugged.

"I have a note on that," said McKnight. "It doesn't say so in so many words, but I gather that you tried to bed every coed on the campus. Is that correct?"

"No," countered Riley. "Only the ones who were willing."

McKnight smiled. "I see. And why did you join the Air Force, Major?"

"I thought it might be something I would be good at."

"Fair enough. You flew in the Korean War and shot down four MIGs?"

"Yes."

"Very good. Almost an ace." McKnight rubbed at the wrinkles around his mouth. "Now then, Major. After the war your record was merely average until you managed to wangle an assignment here at Edwards. And from that point on the change was astonishing. There are statements in your file in Washington which indicate that you were one of the most skilled test pilots ever to serve here, that you performed tests with jet aircraft that have never been quite duplicated by any other pilot. Is that correct?"

Riley shrugged. "In some phases, yes."

"You were so good in fact, that you won the most coveted assignment of all—astronaut training. And how long were you in that program, Major?"

"Five months."

"And then what happened?"

"Don't give me that crap," said Riley, bristling. "You seem to know every damn thing that ever happened to me. So you know what happened at Mercury Beach."

McKnight nodded. "Very tragic. And that seems to be the story of your life, Major. You're either very, very good—or very, very bad. How do you account for that, Major?"

"I don't," said Riley. He stood up and started toward the door. "And if you don't mind, I'm going out for a breath of air. As far as I'm concerned this interview is—"

"Sit down, Major!" McKnight's voice cracked like a pistol shot. "This interview will end when I say it ends! Now listen to me and you'll learn some things about yourself that you didn't know before!"

McKnight waited until Riley was seated again.

"For one thing, Major, did they ever tell you what your ranking in the astronaut program was?"

"No."

"You were No. 11 in the entire program. A fantastic ranking for a man with a background as checkered as yours. Doesn't that ranking surprise you?"

"Yes."

"And I'll tell you something else. Your reflexes tested out at 98.1 per cent, the highest of any man in the program. So all I can say to you, Major, is that you were a fool not to keep your nose clean."

Riley made no comment.

"So be it," said McKnight. "And now we come to the most important part of this interview. And let me warn you, Major Riley, to consider your answers with extreme car. First of all, I must know this. Did you have intercourse with the Exler woman on the beach?"

"Go to hell!"

"Answer the question!" McKnight's voice rose to a shout.

"It's none of your business!" Riley shouted back.

"I warned you that this was important! Do you want to get back into the astronaut program?"

"Yes."

"Then answer the question! Did you have intercourse with Mrs. Exler?"

"Yes, Goddamn it! Yes, I did!"

McKnight's thin face suddenly became calm and he clasped his long hands together upon the desk.

"Thank you, Major Riley. Let me assure you that I am not asking these questions simply to pry. You are, as you undoubtedly know, an uncommonly handsome devil whom the ladies apparently cannot resist. As a result, it is very important for me to determine your exact physical state on the night Mrs. Exler was killed. You had been drinking wine, had you not?"

"Yes. But before we go into that, let's clear up something else, McKnight. Can you get me back into the astronaut program?"

"Possibly, though I have nothing directly to do with the astronaut program."

"Goddamn it! Then why are you giving me all this cock-and-bull about the program?"

"Let me put it this way," said McKnight. "If you perform well for me, if you succeed in fulfilling the mission I have in mind, then I shall recommend you for readmission into the astronaut program."

"Do you pull much weight in Washington?"

"I do."

"All right," said Riley, "let's get on with these questions of yours."

"I have only a few more, Major. I must know the exact physical and emotional state you were in when you struck the blow that killed Mrs. Exler. Now answer me truthfully. Did you panic when you knew she was drowning?"

"I did not."

"With your background, that's probably true. You were tired, shall we say, from your previous exertions, plus the wine?"

"I was relaxed."

"All right. And now here it comes, Major, probably the most important question I'll ask you. Did you, Major Riley, a man with uncommon reflexes, simply miscalculate when you struck that blow?"

Riley gazed directly into McKnight's intense gray eyes. "I don't know," said Riley slowly. "I don't know whether I miscalculated or not."

McKnight folded his long arms across his chest and his elderly face became sober with concentration.

"An honest answer," he said finally. "It is an accepted medical fact that a man tends to lose some of his finer physical co-ordination directly after intercourse. With

27

that in mind, I believe I'm entitled to take a chance on you."

"What kind of a chance?"

"I shall risk my reputation on you," said McKnight. "Will you volunteer for the mission I have in mind—without being told what it is?"

"Yes."

"I knew you would." McKnight glanced at the expensive-looking thin platinum watch on his wrist. "If we leave by jet at two o'clock, we can be in Washington in time for you to meet the board."

There was nothing slow about McKnight once he made up his mind. He allowed Riley twenty minutes to cancel his duty schedule at the base, pack an overnight bag and meet him at the north strip where a four-engine Air Force B-47 was waiting for them.

They arrived in Washington at 9 P.M.

At 9:30 P.M. they were seated in a brilliantly lighted board room in the Pentagon and Riley's second interview of the day was begun.

There were five men on the board. They did not sit behind the room's long mahogany table, but instead collected themselves in a group of comfortable leather armchairs. The identity of the board was not made clear to Riley, nor was he introduced to any of the five men. One of them wore rear admiral's blues, another was garbed in sport clothes like McKnight and the remaining three wore dark, tailored executive suits.

The questioning went on for three hours.

It was the most merciless mental battering and badgering Riley had ever undergone, far more concentrated and detailed than the session with McKnight had been.

Ninety per cent of the questions were directed at him. The rest were directed at McKnight, whom the questioners addressed respectfully as "General." Riley was not surprised; he had decided not to be surprised at anything which concerned McKnight.

At twelve-thirty Riley was told to wait in the anteroom while the board reached its verdict.

A few minutes later McKnight came in with the information. His thin face was subdued and disappointed. "You were rejected," he said.

chapter four

Riley was sent back to California by jet the next day. McKnight remained in Washington.

On Thursday Riley was notified that the general had arrived back on the base and wanted to see him immediately.

A sky-blue command car picked Riley up at noon at the BOQ and drove him deep into the southernmost area of Edwards. After passing through three separate barbed-wire-protected security gates, they reached a small group of freshly painted, two-story buildings.

Riley had flown over this section of the base countless times, but had never paid particular attention to these structures. He saw now why they would be easy to overlook. They were carefully painted the same uninteresting sand color as the surrounding desert, and there were no signs, not even numerical designations, to identify them. All vehicles and aircraft were parked inside the closed hangar building, giving the exterior of the place an unoccupied appearance.

A middle-aged civilian wearing slacks and a tropical sport shirt escorted him to McKnight's office in the small administration building. The office was not large, nor was it well furnished. On the desk was a modest sign, gold letters on black, which stated: *Joseph E. McKnight, Lieutenant General, U.S.A.*

McKnight met him at the door and shook hands. "Congratulations, Riley. You're in."

"Thank you, sir." Riley felt like grinning to show how pleased he was, but McKnight's solemn expression cautioned him. "What happened back there?"

"I had another session with the board," said McKnight.

29

"They approved your entry into the Twelve-Twelve only on condition that I take personal responsibility for your actions. I assured them I would."

"I appreciate that, sir. And what the hell is the Twelve-Twelve?"

McKnight smiled thinly and gestured at the nearby buildings which could be seen through the office's small window.

"You are now looking at the Twelve-Twelve Section, an intelligence division of the United States State Department. But don't let its small physical size and its few personnel deceive you. The Twelve-Twelve's arms reach all over the world."

McKnight stepped over to the desk. "Here are your papers, Riley. Your certification for the Twelve-Twelve and your separation from the Air Force."

"My what?" said Riley.

Glancing at the larger of the two engraved documents, he saw that it was his honorable discharge from the Air Force, dated the previous day.

"Now wait a minute, General!" Riley's voice rose angrily. "I didn't put in for this! And if you think I'll stand for—"

"Shut up, Riley! And learn to control that damn Irish-Latin temper of yours! You're a civilian now, Riley, and you'll remain one until your mission is finished!"

"And then what?"

"You'll be readmitted to the Air Force. If you're still alive, that is."

"I see. And is there anything else I ought to know?"

"A great deal, Riley." McKnight pointed to the door. "Report to Smith across the hall. Former Colonel Smith. And do everything he says, understand? If he says cut off your leg tomorrow morning at six o'clock, you'll do it, understand?"

"Sounds like fun."

They put Riley on the most accelerated schedule he had ever experienced. It began each morning at six and continued for sixteen furious hours until ten at night, including Saturdays and Sundays. The work was so swiftly paced he felt he was earning every cent of his generous salary, which was $2,500 a month. He was in a class with five other men, two of whom were former Navy pilots. Together they crammed detailed courses in Asiatic geography, political science, firearms of foreign countries, rocketry, and advanced intercontinental missiles.

In addition, they were given difficult short-cut courses in Russian and Chinese, taught the rudiments of espionage, including the basic international networks and code structures, and given refreshers in judo and other forms of hand-to-hand combat.

Twice a week Riley was assigned flying missions in a new jet, the fastest he'd ever flown. Designated the F-121A, it was a missile-like aircraft with a long, Coke-bottle-shaped fuselage and short thick wings fronted with massive air scoops for the big J-61 engine. It easily topped Mach 2.3, more than twice the speed of sound. Its ceiling was well over fifty thousand, but he was never able to check it out at that height. His orders were to make speed runs at from fifty to a hundred feet above the flat desert floor and drop football-sized metal capsules on predesignated target areas.

Not once was he given a hint as to what his mission would be. Nor did he meet General McKnight again.

And after five weeks of the training routine he was sick of it, fed up, dying for a chance to get away.

Shortly after midnight one Friday he got out of bed and put on the clothes they'd given him—brown slacks, beige sport short and a garbardine sport jacket. He walked through the darkness to the hangar and told the guard, whom he knew, that he wanted to make a cockpit check on the F-121A. He spent over half an hour checking the instruments and finally the guard grew tired and returned to his station outside the main door.

Riley went to the tool cabinet and obtained the biggest pair of wire cutters he could find. He slipped out a window at the rear of the hangar and walked across the landing strip. There were guards out here also, but he knew their locations and he walked directly to a section of the barbed wire which he knew was well between two patrol points.

He cut enough strands to let him crawl through and then walked a mile through the silent desert darkness to the second fence. After cutting his way through that one, he walked two miles directly south. He had selected this path from the air the previous day, noting it would take him to the only unguarded portion of the third fence. He cut his way through without incident.

He buried the wire cutters in a dry gully, and walked south along two ruts that had been a prospectors' road in the days before the region was acquired by the government. His new freedom filled him with exhilaration and a sense of accomplishment. He walked fast and even ran for a few hundred yards, working up a good sweat.

At dawn he came to an asphalt road and soon he hitched a ride on a Air Force panel truck. When he arrived in the city of Lancaster, he had to wait an hour for the airport to open and then he rented a trim blue and silver Navion and flew toward the dark purple mountains of Nevada.

He reached Las Vegas around ten o'clock, rented a car and drove through the beautiful April sunlight to the Flamingo Hotel. He took a shower, shaved, dressed, and then had two Martinis and a big breakfast of ham and eggs sent up to his room.

And after that he went on the prowl.

He didn't find anything worth picking up in the Golden Nugget or Silver Slipper casinos. But in the Four Leaf Clover his luck promptly changed.

She was a redhead and she was shooting craps with a large, drunken Air Force captain wearing blues which appeared to have been slept in, walked over and driven upon.

Riley strolled closer to the table and decided she was exactly what he needed. Her hair was piled smartly on the top of her head and its copper color was so good it was difficult to tell whether it was natural or dyed. She had saucy green eyes, bright lips, and the freckles across her nose made her look, at most, nineteen or twenty.

Her dress and her actions, however, were those of a woman with considerable experience.

Since Las Vegas was a mecca for Air Force officers, it was probably no coincidence that the dress, constructed of a gleaming metallic material, was an exact shade of AF blue. And it was definitely no coincidence that the dress had an exaggerated V-neckline. Each time she bent over to retrieve the dice, the neckline revealed: (a) that she wore no bra; (b) a great amount of deep cleavage and (c) a greater amount of rounded bosom.

She threw the dice again and failed to make her point.

Riley picked them up. "Allow me," he said. "I feel lucky."

He promptly threw her point—a ten—and she collected fifty dollars.

She squealed with joy. "Nice going, Shooter! Toss 'em again!"

He fired two sevens in a row and she collected a hundred dollars.

"Oh, Shooter," she cried, linking her arm through his. "I think I'm going to like you!"

The captain didn't appreciate the turn events had taken. He glared at Riley with bloodshot eyes that didn't quite focus and drained the last of his whisky and Seven Up. When Riley picked up the dice again, the captain leaned across the table's green surface and slapped them from Riley's hand.

"Shove off, civilian!" he ordered. "This dame's been signed for!"

"Go fry your head," Riley told him pleasantly.

Retrieving the dice, Riley threw an eleven and the redhead shrieked happily as she picked up another double handful of silver dollars.

It was all too much for the captain.

"Shove off!" he bawled, ramming an elbow into Riley's ribs.

It was a big elbow, with plenty of meat and muscle above it, and it knocked the wind out of Riley.

"Goddamn you!" said Riley pleasantly.

He smacked the captain solidly across the eyebrows.

The captain whammed a fist hard into his chest and Riley returned the effort by planting a haymaker exactly on the point of his rubbery chin. The blow knocked the captain backward onto the crap table.

"Hey, Smokey!" he bellowed. "Give us a hand, will you? Hey, Smokey buddy!"

A man rose up suddenly from a nearby divan where he had been dozing. Another captain, in equally rumpled Air Force blues.

He was as big as Captain No. 1 and not nearly as drunk. Leaping off the divan, he launched himself into the air directly at Riley.

This was a mistake because Riley side-stepped easily. Captain No. 2 flew on for a half a dozen more feet, flapping his arms, making a slow aileron roll and part of a Split-S before crashing against the pink asbestos tile. He bounced up full of fight, swearing and shouting, his red-rimmed eyes shining with the eagerness of a man who relished brawling.

He rushed at Riley, both fists swinging, but he did not land a punch. Instead he feinted a couple of times and then delivered a tremendous kick at Riley's legs. It was a well-planned assault. The kick knocked Riley far off balance and while he teetered, almost falling, Captain No. 2 belted him heavily on the cheek and then on the forehead.

Get him, Smokey!" yelled Captain No. 1, still sprawled over the crap table. "Tear him up!"

Riley dodged another blow, found his balance and delivered a thumper against his opponent's nose, producing an immediate spurt of blood. Enraged, the captain scored with a powerful straight right which hit Riley's shoulder and knocked him onto the divan. Instantly the divan upset and Riley land on the floor, shoulder blades first.

He heard the redhead screaming with mixed joy and excitement as the captain once again launched himself into the air. Riley rolled away in time and the man belly-flopped hard beside him, shaking the entire floor.

Still full of battle, the captain raised his head just in

time to get the full benefit of Riley's judo cut. It was not a dangerous cut. But the tough edge of Riley's hand struck his neck with enough force and accuracy to knock him flat onto the floor.

This time, eyes closed, nose bleeding and jaw slack, he did not get up.

Drunken Captain No. 1 promptly roared like an Atlas missile on full power and pushed himself off the crap table. His fists fanned the air harmlessly around Riley's head before he accepted another hard punch on the point of his rubbery chin. Once again he flopped backward onto the crap table.

"Aw, hell, Smokey," he said sadly. "I'm sure disappointed in you."

He slipped off the crap table, struck the floor and was quiet.

The redhead linked her arm through Riley's and smiled up at him, her green eyes shining like crème de menthe.

"Oh, Shooter!" she cried. "You were marvelous!"

With a slam and a crash, two swinging doors opened at the rear of the casino as a pair of muscular bouncers burst in from another room. Grasping the redhead's arm, Riley hurried her out the front door and along the sidewalk.

They celebrated with a round of Golden Fizzes at the Golden Nugget and a round of Silver Fizzes at the Silver Slipper. He learned that her name was Elly Jean and that she had met the two captains after being stranded in Las Vegas by her boy friend, a tech sergeant from George Air Force Base near Victorville. Soon, feeling wonderfully chummy, they drove to his room at the Flamingo. Thirty seconds after the door closed behind them, he slipped the AF blue dress over her head with one hand and slipped her white nylon panties down with the other. She had a nice body, slim-waisted, and her fanny was not much larger than his two palms.

She wasn't as athletic as Fay Exler had been, but she was much livelier than he expected. At first she was like a young mare, squealing and laughing, arching her back,

35

feigning fear of him as she fled to the far corner of the bedroom.

When he came closer, she cupped her hands around her red mouth and pretended to be shouting out the window.

"Rape!" she said, but not too loudly to be heard through the closed window. "Help! Rape!"

"That's one word for it," he grinned.

As soon as he picked her up and carried her to the bed, she pressed her naked breasts against the skin of his chest. Her hands grasped his shoulders insistently, her nails digging deep into his flesh and then even deeper. Her hips began a wonderful rhythm against him. Her green eyes looked up at him boldly, full of desire and excitement, and then she very deliberately bit deeply into the muscle of his chest, her teeth sharp and demanding.

The pain sent his sensations throbbing and soaring far beyond anticipation. He felt suddenly dizzy, felt his emotions whirling on and on, felt their bodies moving together wildly and furiously to the heights of pleasure.

Not until a long time afterward did she speak.

"Oh," she sighed, still impressed. "You were terrific!"

The rest of the weekend passed in a buoyant alcoholic haze. They visited more casinos, won a lot, lost a lot, and drank a great variety of rum drinks. He remembered returning to the hotel with her Saturday night and again on Sunday, sometime around noon. And after that everything dissolved into slumber.

When he awoke it was night and Elly Jean was lying naked on the bed beside him, still asleep.

He dressed, counted the bills in his wallet and saw that five hundred remained. He put three hundred in her purse and then he left.

He arrived back at the Lancaster airport around 1 A.M. Monday and hired a cab to drive him to Edwards.

He dug up the wire cutters and advanced through the darkness to the strands of the barbed-wire fence, noting that they had been repaired.

Abruptly a flashlight clicked on nearby, bathing him

in brilliance. An armed guard approached and shined the light into his face.

"Riley?" he said.

"Yes."

"Please come with me," the guard said. "The general's been waiting for you."

They drove in a jeep to the main gateway and the guard, an Air Force first sergeant, escorted him to McKnight's office.

McKnight sat stiffly erect behind his desk. He looked tired and he did not speak until the guard departed.

"You violated orders," he said. "I could kick you out of the program."

"Will you?" said Riley defiantly.

"No." Sighing, McKnight leaned back in his chair. "I admire your guts, Riley. And frankly I wish I was thirty years younger and could spend my weekends carousing with redheads in Vegas."

"I see," said Riley. "You had me watched?"

"Of course. And I offer my congratulations. No matter how drunk you became you maintained excellent security." McKnight nodded at the door and his tone became sharper. "Now go get some sleep, Riley, and be ready to leave in the morning.

"For where?"

"Pakistan. You take off at 7 A.M."

⸢ chapter five ⸣

They flew above the weather at forty thousand feet—four F-121A jets without official markings, mothered by a plump-bellied KC-135 jet tanker. Riley flew in the No. 2 position and it was strictly no sweat.

His hangover had been cleared by the first extra whiffs of pure oxygen and for hours on end he relaxed in the compact cockpit on auto pilot, letting the navigators in

37

the big KC plot his course. He cruised easily at five hundred miles an hour, and only occasionally did he see the blue Pacific through breaks in the cirrostratus clouds far below him.

They enjoyed brief rests in Hawaii, Guam and the Philippines and whenever the F-121As grew thirsty between stops they were suckled by the tanker.

Less than forty-eight hours later, they set down on a former British landing strip at Anpur in the foothills of northern Pakistan's Hindu Kush Mountains.

Riley slept for eight hours on a hard mattress in a well-maintained barracks which had housed training squadrons of Hurricane and Spitfire pilots during World War II. The building had polished red concrete floors, and broad windows providing views of an unbelievably super-green valley below the air strip and unbelievably blue mountains looming close to the north. The mountains were obviously an optical illusion; they did not look extremely high, but he knew they were among the highest in the world.

He breakfasted on tea and curried eggs brought to his bed by a middle-aged Indian woman wearing a loose, white sari. She put cream and sugar in his tea, although he preferred it black, and then stood at attention at the foot of the bed. When he finished, she took the tray and departed, still without having spoken a word to him.

After dressing, he joined the other three pilots in the recreation room where an ancient, crank-wound phonograph turned out scratchy music hall tunes sung in somebody's prewar British baritone.

Within fifteen minutes Riley had located the only available source of transportation on the base, an old Austin sedan, and was organizing a wine-women-and-song junket to nearby Anpur, which appeared to be a good-sized town.

"Oh-oh," said one of the pilots as they prepared to get into the car. "I think this mission has just been aborted."

A tall thin figure in a suede jacket came down the barracks steps, halted and looked at them sternly. It was

McKnight and he was accompanied by two aides, one of whom promptly strode to the sedan.

"You others can go," he said. "But not you, Riley. The general wants to see you on the double."

Riley cursed and watched the sedan lurch away without him. Then he joined McKnight on the steps.

"Sorry, Riley," said McKnight, "but I want you completely rested for tomorrow morning. Now let's go in and see what the map looks like."

McKnight led the way to a guarded staff room at the south end of the barracks. He dismissed his aides, locked the room's two doors and drew the window's faded red velvet drapes tightly closed.

"All right, Riley," he said. "I'll lay it on the line for you."

He rolled down a large oilcloth wall map of Asia.

"Here's where we are." He pointed a slender, wrinkled finger to a pink, dog-shaped area of moderate size. "This is Pakistan. You will note that its northern tip is part of a unique corner of the world. Here, within a few miles of one another are located parts of five nations—Pakistan, Afghanistan, India, Russia and China. Do you see the advantage of our location, Riley?"

"Yes. From here a plane can fly easily into Russia or China."

"Very good. But not easily, Riley. Nothing we do any more seems to be easy."

Stepping closer, Riley studied the map. "Where am I going? Russia or China?"

"China," said McKnight. "Specifically, the western province of Sinkiang."

McKnight traced an invisible circle on a shaded orange area of the map. "To be even more specific, you are going to the Takla-Makan, one of China's great deserts."

"Desert?" said Riley. "What in the hell have they got there?"

"A Russian missile base."

"I should've guessed."

"It's called Takla-Ma," said McKnight. "One of the biggest missile bases in the world."

"And what do I drop?"

"I see you've already put two and two together. You will drop an object slightly larger than those you test-dropped back in California."

"What will the object be?"

"Sorry," said McKnight. "I can tell you only that it will not be a bomb. And that's all I can tell you. For your own protection."

"I don't get it. Why?"

"I mean this will not be a simple flight. You will go in as low as possible, under their radar, we hope. You will be unarmed. Your only weapon will be speed."

"What about our other pilots? Will they cover me?"

McKnight shook his head. "No. They were trained as back-up pilots, in case something happened to you in training or on the way over here. They received the same instruction as you, but from the beginning this mission was planned with you specifically in mind."

"I go in alone, is that it?"

"Yes. On the final leg. Does that thought bother you?"

Riley expelled his breath slowly and then grinned. "I'll be frank," he said. "At the moment my stomach thinks I just swallowed a magnum of ice cubes."

"I'm glad to hear it," said McKnight. "Only a fool is afraid to admit fear. I don't think I have to tell you that the missile base will be guarded by swarms of Russian jets. We are deliberately sending you in on May 1 in the hope that the celebration of May Day, the biggest Soviet holiday, will keep a lot of their pilots off duty."

"Very thoughtful." Riley shrugged. "I hope to hell it works."

"It will help," said McKnight. "And we've also come up with something else to give you protection. There will be a second plane accompanying you on part of your mission. It will be a U-2. Are you familiar with that aircraft?"

"I've heard reports about it. High altitude, isn't it?"

"Yes. Extremely high, beyond the reach of any Russian jet. It will be flown by Jack Grandee, one of our more experienced U-2 pilots. He will fly very high and directly over you for part of the mission and it is our hope that his blip on the Russian radar will keep them from noticing you—for many minutes, at least."

"Damned good," said Riley. "How far will the U-2 accompany me?"

"Approximately two hundred miles. Jack Grandee will then turn north and continue on a photography mission across Russia. His mission will be important, but definitely secondary to yours."

"What about my target area?" said Riley. "What will it look like?"

"A good question." McKnight walked to a table where a group of enlarged, black and white air photos were carefully laid out together. "I want you to study these and memorize your drop area thoroughly."

The photos, taken on previous U-2 missions, were excellent, the detail so distinct that Riley could make out individual ties in a railroad track and identify water tanks and chimneys on the roofs of the missile base's many buildings.

The distance from Pakistan to the target area was estimated as slightly over nine hundred miles and total flying time was set at no more than an hour and thirty minutes. The target was a desert marsh, approximately twenty miles southeast of the base. Darker in color than the surrounding arid land, the marsh was shaped roughly like an arrowhead.

"You must make your drop exactly here." McKnight placed his finger on the tip of the arrowhead. "And I mean *exactly*. Your margin of error must be less than a hundred feet."

After the briefings, the rest of the day passed slowly. The evening was better, dragging less because the other pilots returned from town and Riley played poker with them until eleven-thirty. He went to bed for four hours, managed to sleep for two and arose at 3:45 A.M.

The airfield was still velvety black when he made his pilot checks of the F-121A, accompanied on the walk-around by McKnight and two ground crewmen.

In the flickering glow of the crewmen's flashlights,

McKnight's wrinkled face looked extremely tired and he seemed to have aged another ten years. But his grip was strong as he shook Riley's hand.

"Listen to me once more," he said. "I know I don't have to tell you this, Riley, but your mission is one of the most vital we've planned in years. We can only make this particular flight once, due to circumstances which are beyond your control and mine. So for God's sake, Riley, be careful."

"I'll do my damnedest," said Riley quietly.

He took off at exactly five o'clock, using the afterburner, and the F-121A slammed him hard against the back rest as it shot into the black, moonless sky at a steep angle, the slipstream hissing like water against the canopy. At fifty thousand feet he leveled off, checked his clocks—tachometer, tail-pipe, temperature, fuel and oil pressure—and all were normal.

At 5:09, exactly on schedule, the pale green blip of the U-2 appeared on his radar screen.

Riley reduced speed to 450, matching the slower rate of the U-2. Invisible to each other in the darkness they flew northeast together, separated by the ten thousand feet between them but united by their instruments.

Soon the rising sun spread a film of salmon pink across the sky and Riley saw the massive peaks of Mount Muztagh stabbing up cleanly through the cloud layer. Because of the clouds, he could not see the rest of the great Chinese ranges but he felt their high presence.

Within a few minutes he was beyond the mountains. He peered through the top of his plexiglass canopy for a final time, trying to spot the U-2 in the brightening daylight. He thought he saw a tiny long-winged object directly overhead, but he couldn't be sure and there was no more time for gazing.

It was 5:30, time for them to separate. Riley pushed the stick forward and the F-121A went into a sharp dive. Very quickly, with just a slight shuddering of the airplane, he passed Mach 1, the speed of sound, and a few moments later he was traveling well over a thousand miles an hour. He held her at that speed, piercing the heavy cloud cover, streaking through it blindly, eyes intent on his instruments—and then he broke into clear morning daylight.

Now he could tell exactly where he was. Behind him were the shadows of the great mountains, the Karakorams. Directly below was the flat, dirty beige color of the Takla-Makan Desert.

He leveled out. When he was five hundred feet above the desert, he debated going lower, because now that he was this close he could see that it was not nearly as flat as it had appeared from above and on McKnight's maps and air photos. He saw gullies, high yellow dunes, hills and higher outcroppings of wind-picked rock.

He decided to risk going a hundred feet lower. And then he rammed the throttle full forward and the airplane leaped ahead as if kicked in the tail by a giant foot.

Now he felt the full exhilaration of his profession, the magnificent power of it, the unlimited speed. The mach-meter passed 2.0, twice the speed of sound, and went further.

He held it at sixteen hundred miles an hour. He held it there minute after minute. His touch was good and he was able to maintain altitude slightly above four hundred feet. Never before had he flown so low and so fast simultaneously. Never before had he known such a glorious sensation of speed. The desert surface blurred past like a rushing river of yellow-brown water.

He held the speed for nineteen minutes. The cockpit became very warm and he felt perspiration running down his cheeks and collecting on the neck of his pressure suit.

Soon he saw directly ahead a range of rough bluish mountains—the Tien Shan—which marked the end of the desert.

He cut speed sharply to one thousand, then five hundred. He climbed higher, high enough to get his bearings. Then he saw it. The missile base, Takla-Ma. It was a vast, irregular affair of sprawling buildings and telemetering towers not far from the foothills.

He looked for his target area, but could not find it.

43

Again he glanced at the missile base and he saw that McKnight's plans to foil their radar had worked. There were no other airplanes in the sky.

Although he didn't wish to, because of the danger of being noticed, he climbed higher. And now he saw the marshes. There were two of them, near a dry sandy river bed.

As soon as he identified the arrowhead-shaped one, he dived toward it. He went down very low, to seventy-five feet, then fifty.

He saw the cloud of sand when he was about a quarter of a mile from his target. The sand was being lifted by a broad, high whirlwind which spiraled along the dry river bed.

He cursed as he and the perverse whirlwind reached the target area at the same time. It took him only seconds to pass through the dirty air, but they were precious seconds of lost visibility, and when he flew clear of the yellowish dust he saw that he had missed the drop area by several hundred yards. *No more than one hundred feet*, McKnight. had warned. *You cannot miss the drop area by more than one hundred feet.*

He was sure there would be time for another pass, even more if necessary.

He used the air brakes to reduce speed as much as possible, but even so his forward rush carried him four or five miles beyond the marshes and much closer than he wished to the missile base.

As he began his wide sliding turn, he was astonished to see two Soviet airplanes climbing into the air a few miles away.

It was impossible. Only seconds before, that part of the sky had been empty.

Abruptly two more swept-wing Soviet jets rose low in the air near the base. On the ground below them he saw puffs of something whitish which dissipated too quickly to be smoke. It was steam. And it explained how the jets had risen into the air so quickly. They were being launched by steam catapults which ringed the base.

He completed his turn. But as he raced back toward

his target area, two more Soviet jets catapulted·up from the desert floor between him and the marsh. Like the other four, they appeared to be MIG-25s, an advanced, long-bodied intercepter capable of very high acceleration.

Because of his turn, he had lost his speed advantage. He rammed the throttle to 100 per cent and began his dive toward the marsh. He felt the Soviet jets begin to hem him in—four behind, two directly ahead. When he was still several thousand yards from his target, they began firing rockets at him.

The rockets were streaks of bluish-white smoke darting across the sky. One shot directly beneath him. Another exploded directly in front of him and as he flew into its concussion the F-121A was thrown violently upward. Even through the protection of his helmet, the force of the blast was tremendous. He was slammed hard against his seat and then jerked forward in his harness.

The F-121A went straight up before falling over on its back. He was astonished that it was still in one piece and still responding to his control. He tasted blood in his mouth and realized vaguely that he had bitten his tongue. For a few moments, he flew upside down and then he righted the airplane with a quick snap roll.

He found himself flying toward the missile base, and he was aware that the rocket blast had helped him perform a maneuver which could not have been accomplished under normal conditions. The four pursuing jets had passed beneath him during the flip-over and were now going in the wrong direction. The other two jets, however, were closer to him than before.

A streak of bluish-white smoke shot beneath his right wing. Another close miss. He decided to dive toward the missile base, hoping they would hesitate to fire their rockets if there was a chance they might accidentally destroy launching pads or fuel centers.

He reached the base. He was traveling in a shallow dive at close to seventeen hundred miles an hour and was about nine hundred feet up when the rocket hit. Even though he had sensed fully the peril he was in, he hadn't really thought it could happen.

The rocket struck his right wing with a crashing detonation and broke it off. Instantly the F-121A began to corkscrew erratically and Riley lost all understanding of balance and direction. The airplane shuddered as if whirling inside a tornado and began to break up.

He knew he was doomed if he stayed with the ship. But at this speed he was also doomed if he ejected, because the air itself would tear him to pieces.

He counted as slowly as he dared. *One, two, three . . .* He felt the other wing snap off and he knew he wouldn't have a chance if the engine blew now. *Five, six, seven . . .* He wanted desperately to press it now, this instant. *Nine, ten . . .*

He pressed the lever under the arm rest.

Everything seemed to explode at once. As the seat carried him outward, the fuselage broke up in large pieces all around him. He was still traveling at least a thousand miles an hour and when he hit the air it was like running headlong into a steel wall.

His body was buffeted by enormous unseen forces. He saw debris boiling past his eyes—a geyser of clear jet fuel, part of the canopy and something which looked peculiarly like a beige-colored stone. Then the screeching wind tore his helmet off and after that he saw only a blood red color because the wind was ripping at his eyelids.

The pain lasted only a few seconds before it and everything else vanished in a wave of darkness and consciousness left him.

⊸⊸⊰ *chapter six* ⊱⊷⊸

For the first twenty-four hours Riley was in such extreme agony that he didn't know where he was and didn't care. Temporarily he was blind, his eyes swollen completely shut, feeling like two large rotten pieces of fruit plastered against his head. The lids were torn and bruised and the slightest movement of his head sent red balls of pain vibrating through his brain. His eyes were so bad he scarcely felt the other damage caused by the buffeting of his fall. His left ankle was sprained, ligaments appeared to be torn in one shoulder, his neck was stiff and his entire body felt bruised from his throat to his knees.

Late on the second day, the medications began to help. His left eye remained tightly closed, but the other one opened slightly, permitting him to see his surroundings through blood-caked eyelashes.

He was not surprised to discover he was in a cell. Its walls, floor and ceiling were rough-cut yellow sandstone, and there were metal bars, either iron or steel, on the long, narrow glassless windows. He felt a breeze from the windows, a movement of cool, dry air which seemed to soothe his swollen throat and nasal passages.

Turning, he saw that he lay on a wooden cot furnished with a thin straw mattress. His pressure suit and wrist watch had been removed and he wore wrinkled trousers of faded blue-green cotton and a shirt of the same thick rough material. The shirt was too small for him and both garments were badly in need of laundering, reeking with a mixture of perspiration and medicine.

Moving his head slowly, to keep the pain at a minimum, he was able to look out the nearest window. Because of the state of his eye, the view was hazy and difficult, but he saw the spidery edge of a telemetering antenna which told him all he wanted to know. He was in a building somewhere on the missile base. Takla-Ma.

He closed his eye. He wished he could blot out his thoughts of what had happened as easily as he shut off the view of the base. It was unbelievable. He shouldn't be here; he couldn't be here in this strange place, thousands of miles from home on the wrong side of the world.

Was it possible that only a few days ago he'd been living it up in Las Vegas? Was it possible that only a day or so ago he'd felt so good, so right, convinced his mission would be a success and he'd win reassignment to the astronaut program? What a dreamer he'd been!

He tried not to think about McKnight, but it was impossible. McKnight had done everything for him. McKnight had given him a chance to prove that he could do something vital, given him a chance to overcome the disaster with Fay Exler at Mercury Beach.

And he had failed.

He had failed himself. But worse than that he had failed the only man who had ever really believed in him.

He clamped his teeth hard together, discovered they ached as badly as the rest of his body, and tried to concentrate on the voices which were arguing somewhere nearby.

They were male voices and they spoke in Russian. One, the most insistent, spoke with a Chinese accent, making it additionally difficult for Riley to understand.

They argued violently and the Chinese voice repeated one word several times.

"*Egolka!*" he said. "*Egolka!*"

"*Nyet! Nyet!*" said the other man. "No! No!"

They began to use medical terms, such as "prescription" and "antiseptic," and Riley became more confused. For a moment he thought they were doctors, but then they began to swear at each other and he became convinced they were not medical men.

Once more the word "*egolka*" was used by the Chinese voice and this time, because of the other phrases they used, Riley recalled its meaning. "*Needle.*" They were arguing about whether to give him an injection of something.

Abruptly the argument ended.

Riley heard a key turn in a heavy lock and then the door to his cell opened. He did not move his head to see who was entering because that would have brought additional pain. He waited until the man came close enough to the cot to be seen through the slit of visibility permitted by his right eye.

The man was Chinese. He was tall for a person of his race, probably five feet ten or better, and he wore a uniform of drab mustard-colored cotton which buttoned tightly around his neck. He was badly in need of a haircut. A hank of straight black hair hung across his broad bumpy forehead which sloped back almost like that of a Neanderthal man. But there was nothing Neanderthal or dull about his shiny black eyes. Partly concealed by heavy Oriental eyefolds, they were intelligent eyes, alert and curious.

As he came closer to the bed, Riley looked at his hands, noting that he did not hold a hypodermic syringe.

"Howdy, fellow," the man said in casual English. "Feeling better, I hope?"

Riley nodded slightly.

"Might as well tell you who I am," the man said chummily. "I'm Colonel Lu Fei-tzu, boss of Chinese Intelligence, but you can call me Lu for short."

He laughed, displaying large brown-stained teeth, and seemed faintly disturbed when Riley did not join in the laughter.

"Maybe you'd like to be less formal and call me George," he added. "That was my handle back at UCLA. Good old George Lu, I was known as."

So far as Riley was concerned, Lu was overdoing it. But he could not help being impressed with Lu's linguistic skill. The man was a peculiar contradiction. From his long pointed fingernails to his smooth beardless chin, he was thoroughly Oriental and yet he spoke American slang as easily as a native of Hollywood and Vine.

"Yeah, I'm an old Bruin," Lu said. "Graduated from UCLA back in 'forty. That makes us fellow alumni, doesn't it?"

Riley nodded.

"My God," said Lu, "is that the best you can do? Come on, warm up a little. I'm not going to hurt you."

Riley pointed to his throat.

"Hurt when you talk?" said Lu.

Riley nodded.

"O.K., O.K.," said Lu, "you don't have to say much. One good answer's all I want from you."

49

He sat on the side of the cot and drew some cigarettes from the breast pocket of his tunic.

"Want one?" He held the package up so Riley could see the picture of a dog on it.

Riley nodded.

"They're Laikas," added Lu. "Russian. Named for that damn pooch in the rocket." He grinned. "Lousy cigarettes. Taste like dog manure."

They lit up. The tobacco was not so bad as Riley expected, stronger than American varieties with a distinctly weedy aftertaste.

"All right, Riley," said Lu, "I'm going to level with you."

Leaning forward, he let his voice drop to a more personal tone. "You're in a hell of a spot, Riley. You came in here in an unmarked civilian plane, obviously on some kind of a spy mission. You're damned lucky to be alive after what those Russian planes did to you. Did you know your 'chute didn't open until you were about a hundred feet from the ground?"

Riley shook his head.

"And when it did open it was nothing but rags. I don't know how it ever held you up. And I guess I don't need to tell you your plane came down in about a million pieces."

Lu dragged deeply on the cigarette, coughed, and made a face.

"Sure wish you'd brought more American cigs," he complained. "One lousy pack. And Fedotov beat me to 'em." He wiped his mouth with the back of his hand and then scowled. "I guess you don't know who Fedotov is, do you?"

"No."

"Colonel Fedotov, U.S.S.R. A very nasty character. He's the head of the KGB Security Committee for the base. He's got the same rank as me but is my superior. That's the way it is around here. The Russians built Takla-Ma and they run it—with our help, of course." Lu placed a long yellow fingernail between his brown front teeth and dislodged a particle of tobacco. "Let me give

50

you a hint about Colonel Fedotov. He'll have you shot if you don't come through with the right answers pretty soon. He's the one that started you on the sodium amytal while you were still unconscious. You know what that stuff is, don't you?"

"No."

"Truth serum. He kept asking you for the name of your collaborator."

Lu leaned closer and breathed cigarette smoke past Riley's face. Riley shut his good eye, not because of the smoke, but because he didn't want Lu to sense in any way that he was disturbed by the fact that they had used truth serum on him.

"And that wasn't all he asked," said Lu. "He wanted to know what you dropped from the plane."

There was a moment of uncomfortable silence.

"You didn't tell him," said Lu. "You didn't tell him anything important—and, man, did you make our boy Fedotov mad!"

Lu laughed so hard the hank of hair fell into his eyes. He brushed at it impatiently, but it remained hooked across his sloping forehead like a small black scythe.

"As I told you," he said, "I'm trying to level with you, Riley. Frankly, I hope you'll tell me the name of the other agent, so I'll get the credit for it, instead of Fedotov." He paused. "How about it? You want to tell me?"

Riley shook his head.

Lu did not appear to be disappointed. "Aw, come on," he said. "You wouldn't hold out on a fellow alumnus, would you, old buddy?"

Riley shook his head. He immediately regretted the movement because Lu's broader grin indicated he had interpreted it as meaning Riley was ready to come through with some facts.

He decided the time had come to test his bruised vocal chords. He spoke slowly. "Don't know . . . any agent. Never told about . . . one."

Lu reduced his grin to a small smile. "I hate to tell you this, old alumni buddy, but I think you're lying."

"No . . ." said Riley. "I know of no . . . other agent."

Lu continued to smile, but now there was no warmth in it. And his next words revealed that he could drop his role of the casual, slang-speaking college man as easily as he dropped ashes from his cigarette.

"How stupid do you think I am?" he said crisply. "You flew nearly a thousand miles to get here. You risked your life to drop something on or near this base. You told us that much when you were under the influence of the drug. Now do you think I'm so stupid I can't guess that you were dropping something for another agent, a person undoubtedly working secretly on this base? Think about that, Riley, and maybe you'll see it the way I do."

Lu tapped some dust off his red epaulets and then folded his arms across his mustard-colored tunic.

"Well?" he said.

"Go to . . . hell," said Riley.

"You're being hasty." Lu's smile was definitely icy now. "You're not thinking, Riley. Do you want me to advise Colonel Fedotov to give you another dose of truth drug?"

"I don't care . . . what you . . . do!"

"Very well," said Lu. "You're asking for it."

Striding to the cell door, Lu struck its solid surface impatiently with his fist. It was opened by someone on the outside, probably a guard, and Lu spoke in Russian.

"Fetch Colonel Fedotov," he said. "At once!"

Then he spoke to someone else who apparently had been waiting in the corridor.

"It is time," he said. "Go in and prepare the patient. I shall wait for Comrade Fedotov."

Riley heard light footsteps and turned his head painfully toward the door.

A girl entered. She was an Oriental, possibly twenty years old, more likely eighteen or nineteen. She wore a white cotton nurse's uniform and carried a white metal tray on which rested a syringe and several small bottles of clear liquid.

"Good afternoon, sir," she said in careful English.

She came closer to the cot and Riley saw that she was distinctly lovely. She was dainty, small-boned and small-breasted and it was difficult to distinguish her nationality. She was not Chinese; more likely she was Indian or Iranian. Light ivory in colory, her complexion was fine-textured and without make-up. She had beautiful natural eyebrows, large brown eyes, and her dark straight hair, parted in the middle, was combed back sleekly and abundantly.

"Are you feeling better, sir?" she asked.

"Don't call him *sir!*" snapped Lu from the open doorway. "Call him prisoner."

"Yes, Colonel." She bowed toward Lu and then turned back to Riley.

"How are your eyelids, Mr. Prisoner? May I—"

"Judith!" exploded Lu. "Not *Mr.* Prisoner! This man has no title. He is nothing. He is lower than low!"

She bowed once more in Lu's direction and then applied a pad of gauze to Riley's right eye. The gauze smelled sharply of alcohol and she daubed it gently against his lashes, removing some of the caked blood and improving his vision.

"Prepare his arm," ordered Lu. "I feel certain that Colonel Fedotov will want him to have another dose."

Her fingers were cool and pleasant as she rolled up Riley's sleeve. She cleansed the skin of his upper arm with alcohol and then stepped away from the cot and looked expectantly toward the doorway.

Abruptly there was the sound of heavy boots coming up a stairway and then along the corridor.

Lu bowed and spoke to a man who replied in booming, gruff Russian.

They talked for a moment before moving further into the corridor, almost out of earshot, where they began a heated discussion. At once Riley was aware that these the same voices he had heard arguing before—and again the subject was the same. He heard the word *"egolka"* mentioned once more, plus several other medical terms in Russian.

In a moment Lu returned to the cell and his dark eyes glittered with victory.

"It is decided," he said. "Please enter, Colonel Fedotov."

Lu bowed very correctly from the waist.

The sound of the heavy leather boots came closer and then the doorway was filled with the bulk of an enormous man.

And as the man came into the cell, Riley was repulsed by what he saw.

⌒⌁(chapter seven)⌁⌒

Colonel Fedotov was fat. He was a tower of disgusting obesity, well over six feet tall and far more than that in circumference. His fat-swollen mammaries protruded against his saffron-colored officer's tunic, bulging his rows of ribbons and medals, wobbling as he walked.

He wore a stiff-brimmed, yellow barracks cap at the proper military angle, a solitary red star gleaming above its patent leather bill. But the cap was the only militarily correct item upon him. His pink chins hung over his collar like untrimmed suet. His stomach, shoulders and upper arms were of fantastic size, making it necessary for his tunic to be of tentlike proportions. His black trousers were equally oversize, flaring absurdly at the sides, stuffed into huge black leather boots which reached nearly to his knees.

"Ah, yes," he said in harsh, throaty English. "Prisoner Riley is awake, I see."

As he moved into the room, his boots creaked from the effort of supporting his weight, which Riley was sure must be over three hundred and fifty pounds. In one hand he carried half of a large Persian melon, in the other a steel spoon. He helped himself to a large mouthful of the orange-colored meat, swallowed noisily and then

54

smiled at the young nurse who was gazing at him uneasily.

"Good afternoon, Judith," he said. "How is my *kro-leek* today?"

Riley wasn't certain what the Russian word meant, but Fedotov's tone and his next gesture indicated that it was probably a term of affection.

As he passed the girl, his large hand touched her back and then slid familiarly down to her hip. She stepped away skillfully and Riley could tell from her quick frown that she was used to such treatment and didn't like it.

Fedotov laughed, strode to a wooden partition on the far side of the cell and stepped behind it. Riley heard a lever being operated, followed by the sound of water flushing and then Fedotov reappeared, his face displaying a vast, cheeky smile.

"Good!" he boomed happily. "Toilet is working. Very good!"

He walked to the tray which the girl had left at the foot of the cot and picked up the hypodermic syringe. Holding it up to the light, he examined the clear fluid it contained.

"Which?" he said. "No. 2 or No. 1?"

"No. 2," said Lu.

"Good," said Fedotov. "No *parrie stahreek?*"

"Correct," said Lu. "No *parrie stahreek*. It is No. 2."

Nodding vigorously, Fedotov handed the syringe to the girl and then made a jabbing motion in the air with an extended forefinger.

"Now," he laughed, "let us see if our pig can squeal."

The girl approached the cot.

Fedotov approached also, taking up a position near her left side, while Lu came closer on her right.

Riley wanted to resist, to fight at least a little and make it hard for them, but there was no strength in him. His legs were heavy with pain and fatigue and as the needle entered the flesh of his arm he wondered what would happen if he tried to roll over and pull his arm away.

Nothing, he decided. They would simply hold him down and start over again.

"You bastards," he said.

Fedotov laughed. "Well, well. Our pig can speak. And he can—"

Riley did not heed the rest of Fedotov's words. He was suddenly aware that the girl was saying something to him, saying it soundlessly, her lips forming the words in English.

"*It is all right*," her lips said and he realized that the two men were ignorant of what she was communicating because they stood behind her.

He had no idea what she meant. He was certain her reassurance had something to do with the injection, but before he could think it through the drug began to make him drowsy. Gradually he felt an easing of the pain in his neck and legs and then he entered an unnatural stage in which he was suspended halfway between sleep and wakefulness.

He could not keep his eyes open and he felt his head fall back loosely against the straw mattress.

"Good!" boomed Fedotov. "You may begin, Colonel Lu."

"Thank you, sir," said Lu's voice. It seemed to come from far away, although Riley knew he must be standing near the cot. "Prisoner Riley, give me your full name."

"Alfred Coronado Riley," said another voice, hollow and strained, and Riley realized vaguely that it was his own.

"Can you tell me the name and rank of the man who sent you here?"

Wanting desperately to resist, Riley tried to shut the question from his mind, but his voice betrayed him.

"Joseph McKnight," his voice said calmly. "Lieutenant General, United States Army."

"Very good. And now think carefully, Prisoner Riley. Can you tell me the name of your collaborator on this base, the name of the person who awaited your arrival?"

"No."

Lu cursed and Riley felt the cot shake as if it had been kicked.

"Be calm," said Fedotov. "He may not know."

There was a pause while they discussed the phrasing of the next question.

"Very well," said Lu. "What did you drop from your airplane?"

Riley did not reply and Lu swore in a mixture of Chinese and Russian.

"State it another way," suggested Fedotov. "Prisoner Riley, what was it that fell from your airplane?"

"The wing."

"What else?"

"The fuel."

"What else?"

"The canopy."

Lu grunted with dissatisfaction. "That's no help. He's telling us how the plane exploded."

"What else?" persisted Fedotov.

Riley did not reply. His mind still teetered between unconsciousness and wakefulness, but he could feel the desire for sleep becoming stronger.

"What else fell from your plane?" said Fedotov.

"A stone."

"What?" Now it was Fedotov's turn to curse. "Did you say stone?"

Riley felt too sleepy to reply.

"It's the drug," said Lu. "It's distorting his mind."

"Stone?" demanded Fedotov. "Did you say stone? Wake up!"

Riley felt strong hands seize his shoulders and begin to shake him. He felt his head rolling from side to side.

"Wake up! Wake up!"

The hands treated him more roughly, knocking him hard against the cot's wooden frame.

"Another dose!" ordered Lu's voice and it seemed to be shouting at him from a thousand miles away. "Quickly, Judith!"

He felt something flick against his arm, but there was

57

no needle sensation, no feeling of pain. He heard them talking excitedly among themselves, the girl's voice, the voices of the two men. Their words began to speed up, chattering and squeaking unintelligibly like a tape running too fast on a recorder. And then he plunged into full unconsciousness.

When he awoke, he was aware that he had slept for a long time. The sharp-edged shadows of early morning were prominent on the cell's sandstone floor and walls, and he realized at once that his eyes were no longer so badly swollen. He moved his head, saw that he was alone in the cell, and discovered with tremendous relief that there was less pain and stiffness in his neck and limbs.

Leaving the cot, he walked to one of the narrow barred windows and looked out. He was not prepared for what he saw. His cell was in a tower, at least five stories up, making escape difficult, if not impossible. Looking out across the base, he could see that it was much larger than it had appeared from the air.

Takla-Ma stretched for miles across the flat, beige-colored desert—complexes of yellow sandstone buildings with heavy slanting roofs of yellow and green tile, irregular networks of streets and dirt roads, radar towers made of flimsy-looking bamboo, and squat concrete blockhouses with pyramidical roofs.

Most impressive of all were the missiles, scores of them everywhere on the base, all sizes, some upright and ready for firing from their huge steel towers, others on trucks and rail cars, still others partly hidden in their ground silos.

Grasping the window's iron bars, he pulled with all his strength and discovered they were sunk deeply and firmly into the sandstone. There were two other long narrow windows in the cell. One was on an exterior wall and gave another view of the base. The other opened into an adjacent cell which was unoccupied. He tested the bars of both, yanking at them angrily, trying to twist them in their sockets, but they resisted each effort.

He returned to the first window and looked more closely at the nearby buildings, some of which were under construction. He saw that the ground around them was littered with chunks of yellow or beige-colored sandstone. The stones were used for the buildings' walls and also as a road surface. And now it made sense. His vision hadn't been distorted by the explosion of the airplane.

He *had* seen a beige-colored stone in the air. And that stone was undoubtedly the most important part of the mission. It was the object he was supposed to drop on the dry marsh. Chosen to resemble other stones on the desert, McKnight's stone would have lain unnoticed and untouched until picked up by the person or persons for whom it was intended.

McKnight had been very wise. From the beginning he had known that Riley might be captured and subjected to truth drugs—and that was why he had withheld the information about the stone and its purpose. But even McKnight hadn't been able to foresee the possibility that the disintegration of the airplane would reveal the stone's presence. And that split-second glimpse had pressed the stone's image deep into Riley's subconscious—but unfortunately not deep enough to resist being drawn out by his captors' drugs.

He heard the heavy lock operating and returned to his cot before the cell's iron door swung inward. A guard appeared, a tall Oriental in a shaggy fur cap, with many bandoliers of rifle ammunition crisscrossing his chest.

Behind him appeared the petite nurse, Judith, carrying a tray of food and medical articles.

Dismissing the guard, she waited until the door closed and then she gave Riley a smile which seemed genuine in warmth and youthful friendliness.

"Good morning," she said in careful English. "You are improved, is it not so?"

"Yes."

"Can you eat?"

"I'd like to try."

She placed the tray on the cot and removed the lids from two clay bowls, revealing a gray potato porridge and green tea. Her small hands moved gracefully, rearranging the dishes for his convenience, and then she stepped back and watched him consume the porridge, which was not as tasteless as it looked.

"Are you not curious?" she said.

"About what?"

"About the good treatment you are receiving. About the fine cell you occupy. You are a very important prisoner, you know."

"No," he said, "but I am curious about you."

At once she lowered her eyes and became silent and he was impressed by the faint shadows her long lashes cast on her cheeks. But at the same time he wondered if her shyness, which seemed a natural part of her, could be part of an act.

"Aren't you afraid?" he said. "Isn't it dangerous to be alone in the same room with an enemy like me?"

"I am not afraid. The Khams are near."

It was not the answer he had hoped she would give.

"The Khams?" he said. "Who are they?"

"The guards." She nodded toward the closed door. "Mountain men from Mongolia. They are fine fighters."

"I suppose they are. But aren't you afraid I might attack you before they could come in?"

"No."

Sipping the fragrant green tea, he looked at her across the rim of the clay bowl, trying to guess what was in her mind. There was no doubt in his own mind that she had tried to reassure him about something while she was giving him the first injection, but he could not guess why. It was not reasonable to believe that she would take his side against Fedotov and Lu, but the thought was worth exploring.

In the past he had always found that the direct approach worked best with women. He decided to try it again.

"Judith," he said quietly, "tell me a little about yourself. For example, you're not of Chinese birth, are you?"

She shook her head.

"Are you Indian?"

She nodded shyly.

60

"What part of India are you from?"

"Kashmir."

"Are you married, Judith?"

Instantly her dark eyes looked down at the floor and he saw that she was blushing, her slender throat and high cheeks touched with a light rose color which made her all the prettier.

"I didn't mean to embarrass you," he said. "May I ask something else?"

"I wish—" She hesitated. "I would rather if you—"

"One more question," he said. "Just before you gave me the injection, you seemed—"

Her reaction was astonishing. She flew at him like a startled robin and clamped her small warm hand across his mouth, preventing him from speaking. In her excitement, she spilled the tea on his shirt and knocked the porridge bowl to the floor, cracking it in two.

Her lips came close to his ear.

"Please!" she whispered. "Do not speak about the drug! You will cause trouble for me!"

She kept her hand firmly across his mouth. Then she twisted about and pointed at the cell's opposite wall.

"A listening device," she whispered. "Between the stones. Please be careful!"

He nodded.

"Sorry," he whispered. "I should've guessed."

"Talk about the bowl," she said. "They are listening."

"Damned clumsy of me," he said loudly

"No, it was my fault," she insisted, as loudly. "Let me pick up the pieces."

"No, let me."

But he did not move toward the clay fragments on the floor. And when she tried to step away from him, he placed his arm firmly around her shoulder and tipped her face upward with his other hand, forcing her to look directly into his eyes.

"Why are you helping me?" he whispered.

"I am *not!*"

"What about the drug?"

She tried to escape from his arms, but he held her more tightly.

"I *know* you helped me!" he said. "What did you do to the drug?"

"Yes," she said. "I made sure you were injected with the No. 2, not the *parrie stahreek*."

"Why?"

Once again there was sudden fear in her dark eyes, and twisting her head, she gazed for a moment at the wall.

"Talk about the food or the bowl," she begged. "*Please!*"

He could feel her small body trembling against him. To ease her anxiety, he spoke a few phrases aloud concerning the spilled porridge and then he began whispering again.

"What about the drug?" he said. "The *parrie stahreek*. What does it mean? What is it?"

"Those are Dr. Fedotov's word for it," she said.

"*Doctor* Fedotov?"

"Yes. He is a medical doctor as well as an Army man. Do not be misled by his ugle size and crudeness. He is very intelligent."

"What about the *parrie stahreek?*"

"It is a terrible drug. The words mean *sodium old man*. And it will do that to you—it will injure your brain, give you the shaky, doddering mind of an old man."

"My God," he said. "And that's what Fedotov wanted to do to me?"

She shook her head. "No, not Fedotov. Lu. He is the worst of the two. Colonel Lu wanted me to inject you with the *parrie stahreek*. But he did not want Dr. Fedotov to know."

"That son of a bitch! I'd like to break him into small chunks!"

"Please!" she said. "Not so loud. Colonel Lu will hear you. And he will do terrible things to you."

"Sorry But what about the stone? Did they mention any more about that?"

"I do not know. And please do not ask me."

"All right," he said. "And thank you, Judith, for warning me—and for helping me."

Abruptly she began struggling harder, trying to wriggle from the firm circle of his arms.

"No! I am not helping you! I do not want to help you—"

"But you did, Judith. You are—"

"No! No!"

Her lips curved beautifully as she repeated the words, entirely too delightful to be overlooked. He bent down quickly and kissed her.

She tried to pull away, but he prevented her by placing his hand in the abundant dark hair at the back of her head. And then for a moment of delectable sensation she remained still and her mouth touched his in a way that was unique, different by far from the lips of Fay Exler and the wanton he'd met in Las Vegas. Her lips had a quality of restrained intimacy which made him want to hold her as tightly as possible.

But it was not to be. Her mouth broke away and her small fists began to drum against his chest.

"Oh!" she cried. "Oh!"

He let her go.

"Oh!" she cried. "Why did you do it?"

She backed away from him, arms upraised protectively, her dark eyes very round and brilliant with fear.

"You're like all the men! All the other ones! You want what they all want!"

She called to the guard, the door was opened and she fled outside.

⤙ *chapter eight* ⤚

All morning and all afternoon Riley was an article of curiosity, a quaint American object to be stared at and studied. All during the long day there was foot traffic on the stairway inside the tower and in and out of his cell.

He lay on the cot and stared back at them.

First came Colonel Lu and Colonel-Doctor Fedotov who asked him the same questions as before.

"Do you remember more about our stone?" asked Colonel Lu.

"No," said Riley.

"Of course you do," said Lu. "You told us how it fell from your plane, remember?"

"No."

"It is easy to guess," said Fedotov. "Your stone—if it is stone—will be found by one of our many searchers, perhaps today. It will contain something, instructions perhaps, for your collaborator."

Fedotov and Lu smiled at each other confidently and departed. Later they returned, accompanied by aides who were carefully equal in number and rank—a Chinese Intelligence major, a Russian Intelligence major, a Chinese interpreter and a Russian interpreter. Many similar questions were asked about the stone, many heads nodded thoughtfully and although Riley gave them no new information many notations were made in notebooks.

At noon Judith brought him a tray containing a thick potato soup and a bowl of boiled rice cereal. She gave him some white pills, but refused to talk to him.

In the afternoon the parade was composed of persons of greater rank and importance. Fedotov called in two consulting physicians, including the director of medical services for the base, who advised that the prisoner should remain bedfast for at least two more days.

Other inspections of the cell and its occupant were made by a young Soviet Air Forces general; a middle-aged Russian woman with a mannish haircut who appeared to be a civilian administrator of considerable stature, and a round-faced admiral of the Chinese Navy. They stared at him rudely, and asked the same questions as the others.

Not until dusk did they leave him in peace. He was much improved, feeling so strong that it was difficult to remain on the thin straw mattress and portray a patient whose legs and arms were stiff with soreness.

When Judith arrived with his supper tray, he pushed himself to a semi-sitting position and pretended to vomit weakly into a clay bowl on the stand beside his cot. He retched, groaned, produced nothing and fell back lengthwise on the mattress. But in a moment he pushed himself up a second time and made another weak effort.

"Oh," she exclaimed, "you are very sick!"

At once she rapped on the heavy door, calling to the guard.

"Notify Dr. Fedotov! The patient is worse!"

The guard did not understand her. As soon as Riley heard the key turning in the heavy lock, he rose quickly from the cot. All afternoon he had known he would make this attempt, no matter how impossible it seemed. And he had known he would have to do it tonight, before they tightened their security.

He arrived at the door just as it began to open.

He thrust his bare foot into the opening and at the same time hurled Judith screaming to the floor behind the door where she would be out of the way.

The Kham guard was not prepared for such a burst of energy from a man who had lain ill and unmoving for two and a half days. As the door opened, he took a backward step and for a moment there was puzzlement on his long-jawed Mongolian face. He was extremely tall, at least six foot five, and his large dark hands instinctively raised his long rifle and aimed its metal butt plate at Riley's head.

Riley dived. His hundred and ninety pounds struck accurately against the guard's shanks and it was like crashing into two upright steel rails. For a second, Riley thought he had failed, but then the Kham went down, landing on his side, shouting in a dialect Riley couldn't understand. Riley leaped upon him, struck at the big jaw with his fist and in his anxiety missed it completely. His second blow had all his strength behind it and was on target. The contact with the huge jawbone sent violent

65

shock waves coursing up his arm and then the large man lay silent.

Riley heard shouts and running footsteps and saw another tall Kham guard charging toward him from the doorway at the end of the short corridor.

The second guard halted a few yards away and began to bring his rifle to aiming position.

Riley's reaction required no thinking. He snatched up the rifle from the fallen man in front him, swung it like a bat and released it at the height of its arc. The rifle spun propeller-like through the air, struck the guard's weapon, knocked it from his hands and knocked the shaggy fur cap from his head. As Riley ran toward the man, he saw an expression of astonishment cross the heavy Mongolian features as plainly as if caricatured in ink. His shoulder struck the guard's chest but the man did not go down. Instead Riley himself fell, landing heavily on his stomach.

He picked up the nearest rifle and tried to rise to his knees. The guard knocked him down with a tremendous blow on the head and drew his boot back for a kick. Riley rose swiftly and rammed the rifle's steel butt plate deep into man's groin.

The guard shrieked as if disemboweled. He crouched in pain, clutching his crotch with both hands.

Riley measured the distance to the top of the shaved head and slammed the rifle against it. The man stopped shrieking. He fell doubled up to the floor and lay without moving.

Riley heard a voice calling to him from the cell's doorway. Turning he saw Judith standing there, he face pale and shaken.

"Come back!" she said.

He did not speak to her.

He ran to the end of the corridor and started down a dark stairway. He heard footsteps coming up from below and knew his battle with the two Khams had aroused attention. Despite the darkness he increased his speed and when he met the man on the stairway he had height and surprise as advantages.

He knocked the man down with a single smashing stroke of the rifle. Then, kneeling over the stretched-out figure, who appeared to be a Chinese noncom, he removed the pistol from the man's canvas holster. Discarding the Kham mountain rifle, which was entirely too heavy and unwieldly, he snatched off the man's boots and resumed his dash down the stone steps.

There was high excitement in him now because if he moved quickly enough he might be able to get down from the tower before the other guards became organized. Eyes more accustomed to the staircase's gloom, he took the steps by twos and threes, clutching the boots in one hand, pistol alert in the other.

He reached the bottom of the fourth and last flight of stairs without encountering anyone else. Then he stepped cautiously into a courtyard which was brightly lighted by a row of floodlamps atop a stone wall. He saw two Russian soldiers seated on a bench near the wall. He was relieved to see that they were smoking and talking casually, because it meant the sound of his fight with the guards had not been heard down here. Stepping back into the doorway, he stooped and tried to draw on the boots. He swore quietly. They were too small—at least two full sizes too small.

From the doorway he studied the position of the soldiers in relation to the outside gate and made up his mind quickly. He would walk until they noticed his bare feet and became curious and then he would run like hell toward the gate.

He folded his arms across his chest, concealing the pistol beneath his left forearm, and walked from the doorway.

He watched the two soldiers from the side of his eyes. They did not notice him until he had taken a dozen steps. They looked at him, but continued to talk.

After he'd gone another dozen steps, he was sure they had seen his bare feet, but they remained on the bench and now they were lighting fresh cigarettes. He could not understand it. Surely they were under orders to investigate anything curious or suspicious. And a hatless, barefooted man, over six feet tall, must certainly qualify as an object to be halted and inspected.

But still they made no move toward him. As he reached the gate, which was constructed of wood heavily wrapped with barbed wire, a pair of tall Kham guards appeared and swung it open for him. They grinned at him amiably. One spoke in a Chinese dialect which Riley didn't understand and extended his hand, undoubtedly so he might examine Riley's pass or identity card.

Since he had neither, Riley simply grinned back and kept on walking. He might have gotten away with it—but abruptly a voice shouted down from a window at the top of the tower.

Riley didn't understand the words but he got the message. One of the guards he'd fought with up there had recovered and was bawling orders at the top of his voice.

Riley ran.

He was on firm earth now which gave him good footing and he ran the way he'd been taught in college, calves driving, knees coming up well. He ran beside the wall. He ran straight, without zig-zagging, because he wanted all the speed he could get.

A rifle cracked once, a flat, ugly sound. And then he was no longer a target because he'd reached the end of the wall and turned the corner. He continued to sprint, running in darkness beside another section of wall which was not lighted as the other had been. Stones, twigs and other sharp objects hurt his naked feet but he did not slacken speed. Reaching the end of the second wall, he turned left and ran along a sandy road beside a stone building which was under construction.

He met no one. And it was not reasonable, because from the cell's windows he had seen scores of civilians and soldiers performing tasks everywhere on the base. He ran four hundred yards, five hundred yards, changing course when necessary to remain in the darkness along the stone flanks of the buildings.

When he finally encountered someone, it occurred

swiftly, without warning and at top speed. In the darkness he did not see the sentry until an instant before they collided and by then it was too late. The impact was tremendous. Riley's head smashed into the other man's skull, he flipped upside down in the air and tumbled heavily to earth on his back.

For a moment he could not move and he thought his spine was broken. He knew he should get to the sentry before he began shouting for help, but he felt paralyzed. He could not suck in enough air and his heart and lungs strained as if ready to burst. Through it all his mind remained fairly clear, beset with the irony of what had happened. To get this far and then crash into the only man around wasn't just bad luck; it was the height of stupidity.

When he was finally able to sit up, he saw the sentry lying on his side nearby. Painfully he crawled over to the man, fell across him and seized his throat. Only then did he realize it wasn't necessary. The sentry had been knocked thoroughly unconscious and lay unmoving as if under heavy anesthetic.

He was a Russian soldier, taller than average. Riley pulled off his boots and tried them on. They were snug, but wearable, and he decided the mishap was a good thing after all. He tucked his cotton trousers into the boot tops in the approved Soviet military syle, and then located his pistol which had fallen nearby. He found the sentry's barracks cap, put it on, slid the pistol into his trouser pocket and began walking.

He discovered that his legs once again were extremely sore, the result of the unaccustomed sprinting as well as his tumble. He had no idea where to go, but he knew he had to get farther away from the tower area, which in the last few minutes had burst into activity. He saw searchlights slashing the darkness, heard commands shouted on loudspeakers in Russian and Chinese, heard the clashing of car and truck gears and knew a search was being organized.

He walked around the unfinished building and then passed between two well-lighted structures from which came the thumping sounds of heavy machinery. Soon he came to a cleared area many acres in size and heard an unusual hissing noise and sounds which resembled bubbling water and fire. Off to the side he saw a long narrow concrete platform near which stood a large squat tank on stilts. Beneath the tank could be seen a good-sized flame.

He walked across the field toward the device and as he approached he saw that sentries were posted at both ends. He decided not to go any closer; nor was it necessary to do so. He had seen enough to confirm his thoughts. The device was one of the steam catapults the Russians used to launch jet aircraft from the base. This one unfortunately was minus its aircraft.

He paid it no further attention. Not because he was disinterested, but because he had no wish to arouse the curiosity of the sentries.

When he was midway across the field, he heard a loudspeaker atop a huge nearby building calling out a message which included the word *"obbehd"* several times. His cram course in Russian had been brief but thorough in some respects, and he knew the word meant "dinner." As he walked on, men began to leave the building. At first only a few appeared, but soon scores, then hundreds streamed from numerous doorways onto the field.

In a few moments he was surrounded by moving men. Chinese. Russians. Soldiers. Civilians. And here and there the tall form of a Kham Monogolian. Some picked their teeth, others rubbed grease from their mouths. Some belched. And he knew that all this activity explained why the field and nearby areas had been so deserted previously. The large building was a mess hall and the men had just ended their evening meal.

Some glanced at him, some jostled him as they passed, but none displayed particular interest in his rough uniform. It was easy to understand why. They were the shabbiest, most ragged-assed collection he'd even seen.

Half the Chinese and some of the Russians were without shoes, even though the evening was cool, and this explained why he'd attracted no attention from the tower soldiers when he'd walked past barefooted. Their faded cotton fatigues were patched, dusty and stained with grease, oil and perspiration. In contrast, however, their faces were clean. The Russians wore their hair quite short and many of the Chinese had shaved heads, undoubtedly to minimize the activities of lice.

Riley walked on. He came to a stone-paved thoroughfare which rumbled with heavy truck traffic. He crossed with a group from the mess hall and as they reached the opposite side two small sedans whizzed by, bells clanging on their front fenders, blue lights blinking on their roofs.

The men turned and watched them go by.

"KGB," commented one of the Russians. "Looking for someone."

The others nodded and walked on. Riley stayed with them and he didn't need to have the letters KGB explained to him. That was Fedotov's outfit, the Security Committee for the base.

Soon the soldiers began to separate, going to numerous barracks and other buildings along the way. Finding himself alone and feeling more conspicuous, Riley turned and walked along an unpaved side street which was darker and had less traffic.

A sense of greater urgency was rising within him. He knew he couldn't possibly reach one of the base's outside gates on foot, even if he knew where to find the closest one. The distance was far too great and the longer it took him to get there the easier it would be for Fedotov, Lu and their numerous aides to find him.

He heard brakes squealing behind him and was almost knocked down by a small sedan which turned off the street and cut directly in front of him.

Leaping back, he dodged successfully, his hand tightly gripping the pistol in his trousers pocket. The car resembled the KGB sedans and he was so certain it had arrived to arrest him that he stared with disbelief as it continued for another fifty feet before stopping.

Two Soviet soldiers got out. They did not look back

at him. Singing boisterously, they locked arms and weaved drunkenly toward a single-story stone building from which came the gay sounds of zithers and violins. They entered, laughing about something as they slammed the door behind themselves.

Riley walked on a few steps until he could read part of the Russian letters painted on the door. *Senior Sergeants Club.*

He made his decision at once. He walked to the sedan, which was a rusty Czech model, got in and sat behind the wheel.

But there was no key in the ignition. It was a blow, because he had been certain the soldiers were too drunk to remember to remove the key.

Hoping no one had noticed him, he opened the door to get out and then he noticed the two wires hanging below the small dashboard.

Ignition wires.

His confidence soared as he twisted the bare ends together to make an electrical contact. He switched on the headlights and located the starter knob on the floor near the clutch. The warm engine started at once with a high-revolution howl. He experimented with the stick shift, located reverse and high, and turned onto the street.

He drove slowly for a few minutes, getting the feel of the car, and then he turned onto the stone-paved thoroughfare and joined the truck traffic which was moving rapidly.

It was a superb feeling to be traveling at a good speed, and after covering a half-mile he spotted a sign which filled him with optimism: *North Gate, 22 Kilometers.* With a little more good luck, he could be there in half an hour.

A KGB sedan passed him, traveling very fast, its bell ringing loudly. A moment later, he saw another one, traveling in the other direction. At the next intersection a loudspeaker mounted on a truck shouted commands in Russian and Chinese. He could not understand all the words, but it sounded as if they were ordering the thoroughfare to be cleared of vehicles and pedestrians.

He drove another block. He felt a chill as a second truck loudspeaker shouted loudly, very close behind him.

Up ahead, soldiers stood in the street gesturing at the traffic, shunting the vehicles off the thoroughfare. Riley had no choice. He followed a truck onto a dirt side road and was promptly enveloped in choking yellow dust kicked up by its large rear wheels.

The truck slowed to a crawl. He tried to cut around it and met headlights coming in the opposite lane. He tried to get back behind the truck, but there was no room there now, because another vehicle had pulled in.

He hit his brakes. Immediately another truck pulled up beside him, showering him with dust that billowed in through the sedan's open windows.

As soon as he saw the armed soldiers piling out of the truck, he knew he was trapped.

He tried to get out of the sedan, but the truck was so close the door opened only an inch or two. He threw himself across the seat and got the other door open, but it was no good. Shouting like madmen, two soldiers ran up and slammed the door shut.

There was no time for fear, no chance to make a fight of it. He got the pistol up and put a bullet into the nearest soldier, but then the rifle butts, half a dozen of them, came at him through the windows.

They knocked his arm aside, sending the rest of the bullets into the windshield and roof. They knocked the pistol spinning to the floor and then the steel-plated rifle butts slammed into his belly, his chest and started methodically on his head.

The last thing he saw were the soldiers' grim faces, turning red from their exertion. And the last thing he heard were their shouts and heavy grunts as they pounded him unconscious.

They returned him to the same cell high in the tower, but this time his treatment was different. This time they let him suffer. They did not attend to his new injuries, the deep cuts on his forehead and neck, the bulging contusions on his legs and upper arms. They brought him no food and no water.

The long night passed slowly. In the morning his throat was painfully swollen and dry. He dragged himself from the straw mattress to the toilet and dipped up a tin cupful of water. It was brackish and reeked of sulphur and other minerals but it eased the pain in his throat.

Returning to the cot, he was startled by words spoken loudly from the adjoining cell.

"Mornin', Yank," said a male voice with a nasal British accent.

"Who the hell are you?" said Riley hoarsely.

"Bernard, sir."

"Bernard who?"

"Bernard Shipe. And if you don't mind my sayin' it, sir, you're not only a bloody mess. You're in a peck o' trouble, you are."

Riley did not comment. His aching bones and muscles wanted to remain on the cot, but instead he rose and walked slowly to the barred window between the two cells.

The man on the opposite side was small, bony-shouldered and garbed in rough prison cotton. His face was as narrow as a two-by-four stick of lumber. It displayed two milky blue eyes, a healthy pink and white complexion, a brush of crew-cut red hair, and a tiny mustache of the same brilliant color.

"Let me give you a bit o' warnin'," Shipe said. "They'll be comin' for you in a minute or two."

"Thanks," said Riley. "Where are you from? England or Australia?"

"The latter, sir. Ex-Corporal Shipe, formerly of Melbourne."

"Prisoner of war?"

"Not exactly, sir. I'm in disgrace you might say. Temporarily, I hope."

"Why temporarily?"

Shipe shrugged. "If I do my job properly, they'll let me out."

Quite suddenly Riley decided he didn't like Shipe's attitude. Nor did he like the man's constant and almost sardonic use of the word *sir*.

"And what is your job here, Shipe?"

"I'd rather not say, sir. Not that I don't want to, y' understand. It's just that I—"

Shipe's words railed off into a birdlike squawk as Riley's hands shot between the bars and fastened around his throat. He lifted the small man off the floor and slammed his face against the bars.

"You son of a bitch!" said Riley. "You're a turncoat, aren't you?"

Shipe's mouth opened but no words came out.

"Answer me!" said Riley. "Are you a goddamn turncoat?"

He eased the pressure of his fingers, but Shipe did not speak.

"Answer!" said Riley. "You're here to keep an eye on me, isn't that it?"

"No, sir! Not at all, sir!"

But Shipe spoke too quickly, and his inflection was forced and false. Angrily Riley released him, hurling him away from the bars. Shipe tripped, fell and scrambled to his feet.

"Crummy Yank!" he said, standing a safe distance from the bars. "You'll get yours. Any minute now!"

Riley returned to his mattress and lay down. But his rest was brief, interrupted by voices outside his cell and the unlocking of the door.

Four military aides came in first, followed by Fedotov and Lu.

"Get this man up!" Fedotov ordered. "At once!"

A Russian major and his Chinese counterpart lifted Riley roughly from the cot and forced him to his feet.

Fedotov's voice boomed out as if he were addressing troops on a parade ground.

"Attention, Prisoner Riley! For the crimes of espionage and attempted escape, the sentence is death. Do you have anything to say before the sentence is carried out?"

"Speak!" commanded Lu. "Identify the other spy who awaited your arrival at this base."

"Confess!" said Fedotov.

"I have nothing to say," said Riley. "My God, how many times do I have to tell you that?"

"Very good," said Fedotov. "Prepare the prisoner!"

Lu's chief aide produced a three-foot length of brass chain and bound Riley's wrists tightly behind his back.

They pushed him out the doorway and into the corridor. During the walk down the four dark flights of stone stairs, there was no conversation, and when they stepped into the courtyard, the bright morning sun was like a bomb burst against Riley's eyes.

As he became used to the glare, he noticed that Fedotov and his aides for some reason had not accompanied the others from the building. He heard the sound of marching feet, many of them, turned and saw a dozen Chinese soldiers stepping out briskly across the courtyard's stone surface.

Each carried a blue-steel Tokarev rifle. Their oval-shaped canteens slapped in rhythm against their hips as they turned first left, then right, smartly following the shouted commands of a young Chinese buck sergeant.

The sergeant halted them perhaps twenty paces from the courtyard's stone wall. He shouted again and the dozen men turned so their line was parallel to the wall.

The sergeant shouted another order which vibrated noisily, in and around the neighborhood buildings.

"Ready!"

A dozen rifles came up in unison against a dozen shoulders.

"Aim!"

A dozen rifles aimed at a blank space on the wall.

"Fire!"

A dozen firing pins snapped metallically into a dozen unloaded chambers.

The sergeant ordered the men to lower their rifles and then took up a position of rigid attention beside them.

"Fix the prisoner," ordered Lu.

His aides marched Riley quickly to the wall and fastened his wrists tightly to a metal ring in the stone surface behind him.

Lu folded his arms across his mustard-colored tunic. His brilliant dark eyes studied Riley intently.

"Are you prepared to tell us?"

"No."

"Very foolish," Lu paused thoughtfully. "You are willing to forefeit your life?"

"I don't think it will be necessary."

"What do you mean?" Lu brushed angrily at the hank of his sloping forehead. "Explain yourself?"

"The whole thing's phony," said Riley. "You won't shoot me. You can't afford to."

"Why not?"

"You know why as well as I do. Shoot me and you erase your only possible link with the other agent you claim is on this base. And as long as that other agent exists, the entire operation of this base is under observation."

"You are mistaken," said Lu. "We will find the other agents—and we do not need your presence to lure him out into the open. You are finished, Prisoner Riley. You do not realize it yet, but you will when you see what has happened to your contacts."

"You're nuts," said Riley. "I have no contacts."

"You shall see."

Lu made a brisk about-face and strode to a position beside the firing squad. Reaching inside his tunic, he brought forth a brass-tipped swagger stick which he pointed at the doorway to the tower.

"Bring out the prisoners!" he commanded.

At once there was activity in the doorway. Two men were brought out, their hands fastened behind their backs. They moved sluggishly, stumbling. They were Russian soldiers, wearing the bands of noncommissioned officers on their red epaulets.

"Bring out the others!"

Two more bound men were brought from the doorway. They were the two tall Mongolian Kham guards whom Riley had battled during his escape and they also moved sluggishly, prodded by their escorts.

Lu gestured with the swagger stick.

"Fix the prisoners!" he ordered.

The four men were led to the wall close beside Riley and as their wrists were fastened to the metal rings he realized why they had moved so slowly. All four were drugged, their eyes glassy, their limbs so rubbery they were barely able to stand. And now he recognized the two Russian soldiers. They were the ones who had gone into the senior sergeants club, singing drunkenly, leaving the car parked where it had been easy for him to take it.

Lu strolled along in front of the bound men. He touched one on the shoulder with his swagger stick and prodded another lightly in the stomach. They did not react.

Halting before Riley, he tapped him first on the arm, then on the cheek.

"What do you think of your stupid friends now?" he asked.

"Don't give me that crap," said Riley. "I don't know these people."

"Only half correct," said Lu. "It is true that these blockheads are not your friends—"

He pointed his stick at the tall Kham guards. "They will be shot for incompetance because they let you escape."

He pointed his stick at the two Soviet noncoms. "But this pair is different. They will be shot as confessed traitors. They confessed accepting money from you as payment for allowing you to take their car. They are your contacts—the worst dregs of mankind. The Soviet Union can very well do without their sort."

"More crap!" said Riley. "You know damn well they were drunk. They had no contact with me. They simply—"

"Silence!" said Lu.

"The whole thing's a farce," said Riley. "You pumped these poor bastards full of dope so they wouldn't be able to talk and tell the truth. And if you think you can—"

The brass tip of the swagger stick flashed through the air and struck Riley's mouth so viciously his lip was torn and he tasted blood.

"You will be silent!" said Lu. "You will not speak again until asked!"

He made an abrupt about-face and returned to his former position beside the Chinese soldiers. He spoke in a low voice to the sergeant. The sergeant nodded and spoke to his squad.

Each man removed a clip of ammunition from his belt and snapped it metallically into place in his rifle.

The men waited expectantly.

Lu tapped the swagger stick against his palm.

Two minutes passed.

Five minutes. Ten.

Although the morning sun was still cool, Riley felt perspiration on his forehead and a growing nervous pressure within. He told himself there was no need for it. This delay was so obviously deliberate. It was so obviously part of their pattern, designed to make him sweat, designed to bring him to a psychological state where he would say anything to get relief from the pressure.

But even as he convinced himself of this, a small part of his brain refused to follow the logic. And he knew why. Because there might not be logic in what Lu and Fedotov intended to do. It was possible that the whole setting—the silent courtyard, the four men beside him, the waiting firing squad—was *not* being staged, was *not*

79

a contrivance designed to make him confess. But if that was true, then the alternative was unthinkable.

Ht felt an overwhelming desire to spit the blood from his torn lip onto the ground, but he did not. Instead, he stood straighter, placing his shoulders firmly against the wall.

Finally there was a stirring in the tower doorway as Fedotov's large bulk appeared, followed by several uniformed aides. One of them carried a wooden box which was about a foot and a half square.

Fedotov walked slowly, trying to look as military as possible, but not succeeding because his great stomach and mammaries jiggled with each step. His face wore an expression of triumph and self-satisfaction.

Halting before Riley, he ordered his chief aide to remove the lid from the box.

"Our search was very difficult," Fedotov said, "but successful. Reveal our prize."

The aide tilted the box so Riley could see what lay within. There were two beige-colored objects, each about twice the size of a football. Each was a hollow shell, manufactured on the outside to resemble rough sandstone. Inside each section were maizes of colored wiring, transistors and small batteries, all cushioned on foam rubber. It was clearly obvious that the halves, when fitted together, would form an excellent replica of the kind of stone used in construction of the base.

"A clever device," said Fedotov. "A powerful transmitter. Take it closer so our prisoner can read what is printed on this equipment and confirm its origins."

The aide stepped near enough so Riley could see the brand names on the transistors and wiring.

"Westinghouse, General Electric," said Fedotov. "Fine American firms. Prisoner Riley, do you try to deny that you flew this transmitter to this base, with the intention of letting it fall into the hands of your collaborator."

Riley did not reply.

"I accept your silence as an admission of guilt," said Fedotov. "Now listen carefully, Prisoner Riley, because what I am about to say will not be repeated. This transmitter was not delivered, due to the fine marksmanship of our Russian pilots. But your mission was more of a failure than you yourself are aware. The pilot of the other airplane, the U-2 which flew to conceal your mission, also met with similiar disaster.

"Our rockets brought him down over Russia and he has confessed his part in your plans. In addition, your contacts on this base have confessed their role in your miserable scheme and now stand beside you ready to suffer their penalty. You have been sentenced to death on two counts, for espionage and for trying to escape. In the next minute, you will forfeit your life for these crimes—"

Fedotov paused. It had been a long speech and he was short of breath.

"Prisoner Riley," he continued. "You have heard the charges. You will now be given you final opportunity to reply. Do you have anything to offer? A name perhaps? Do you have a name to offer us in exchange for your life?"

"I do not," said Riley.

"That is your final word?"

"Yes."

"Very good," said Fedotov. "It is done. It is finished."

He motioned to his aides. All of them turned and walked to a position beside the firing squad.

Fedotov signaled to Lu.

Lu made a downward stroke with his swagger stick.

"Ready!" ordered the Chinese sergeant.

The twelve rifles were raised and placed against the soldiers' shoulders.

"Aim!" ordered the sergeant.

The rifles moved slightly, bearing on their targets.

Riley kept his eyes on Lu. He was sure Lu would speak again, in plenty of time to keep the triggers from being pulled. But despite his certainty he felt the skin on his chest begin to crawl.

And then Lu spoke.

"Prisoner Riley!" he shouted. "Attention!"

Riley felt like grinning with relief, but he did not.

"This is your last chance to live!" shouted Lu. "Give us the name!"

"Your final chance!" shouted Fedotov. "Name the agent!"

"Go to hell!" said Riley. "Both of you can go straight to—"

His words were drowned out as Lu made another downward stroke with his stick and the twelve rifles fired.

The concussion from the muzzles was a terrific force against Riley's eardrums and in the first moment he was certain blanks had been fired. But at the same instant he felt a great stuttering impact against the wall which could only be from bullets.

And like tall trees suddenly axed, the two Kham guards bent in the middle and fell forward, hanging from their wrist chains, heads and shoulders downward. Brilliant red stains were on the wall above and behind them.

Before Riley's mind could accept what had happened, Lu brought his stick down again and the rifles fired a second time.

There was the same concussion and impact. Riley felt something wet and red spatter his sleeve and knew what it was.

The two Soviet soldiers slumped from their chains and were still.

It was incredible. Riley stood unmoving, not breathing, his body as stiff and rigid as the wall.

He stared at Lu and knew that if the stick moved so much an inch downward the rifles would fire a third and final time.

The moment was unendurable. The twelve muzzles seemed closer, as if the twelve silent, concentrating riflemen had advanced several steps nearer to the wall. Lu's stick remained poised in the air. Nothing moved anywhere in the courtyard except wisps of pale blue smoke which curled slowly, impersonally, around the rifle barrels.

Lu spoke.

"Prisoner Riley," he said. "Do you now wish to make a statement?"

Riley kept silent. He looked away from Lu. He could not bear to look any longer at Lu's arrogant Oriental face because to look at him made the desire to strangle him impossible to endure.

"Very good," said Lu. "Prisoner Riley, your execution is postponed until tomorrow. You will be given a day and a night to meditate."

There was another moment of silence.

And then, abruptly, a protest came from someone standing beside the firing squad. Astonishingly it came from the throat of Colonel Fedotov, who was looking at the four bodies with eyes transfixed, his great cheeks pale and quivering.

The protest became a roar. And to it was added the shouts of Colonel Fedotov's two aides, who were pointing accusing fingers first at the bodies and then at Lu.

Fedotov advanced upon Lu and his anger seemed to grow with each heavy step.

"Explain it!" he roared, adding several rapid phrases in Russian which Riley couldn't understand.

Lu appeared surprised and puzzled, but even from twenty paces away Riley could see that there was a synthetic quality to his expression.

"Explain it?" Lu said. "But Colonel-Doctor, I carried out your orders. I simply—"

"Idiot!" roared Fedotov. "Fool! Not the soldiers! Not our Russian soldiers—"

Fedotov gave Lu an angry push backward. He shoved him again, harder, and Lu stumbled and nearly fell.

Immediately Fedotov's two aides attacked Lu's two aides, pummeling and kicking them. A Russian and a Chinaman tumbled together upon the stone paving, rolling over and over, hands locked upon each other's throat.

"Enough!" roared Fedotov. "Stop it!"

The scuffling broke off and the two officers regained their feet. Dusting off their uniforms, they glared at one another hotly.

"Fools!" said Fedotov. "Attend to the
move him to his cell."

The two Russian aides came to the wall and unfastened
Riley's wrists from the metal ring. They led him toward
the doorway.

He heard a crackling noise and looked back over his
shoulder. He saw that Fedotov had taken away Lu's
swagger stick and had broken it in two.

There were two sharp slapping sounds as Fedotov
cuffed Lu's cheeks, first with his heavy right hand, then
with his left. One of the aides abruptly struck Riley on
the side of his face, preventing him from looking back.

"Eyes ahead!" he ordered.

They hurried Riley into the doorway.

∽◅(chapter ten)▻∾

During the early afternoon hours, Riley heard sounds
on the base which might have been gunfire. He stood at
the western window of his cell and looked out, but he
saw no unusual activity in the direction from which the
sounds came.

"It's true, Yank!" called Shipe from the adjacent cell,
his nasal voice muffled by the wall. "I believe they're
shootin' at one another!"

"Have you seen anything?"

"No," admitted Shipe, "but I wouldn't be surprised if
they did. Have you seen anything, Yank?"

"No."

Riley remained at the window, shielding his eyes from
the sun, carefully studying the western areas of the base.
It was possible that the gunfire sounds were merely
from a military training exercise somewhere out of
sight. But, like Shipe, he preferred to think the firing
squad incident had provoked other outbursts, other fighting elsewhere on Takla-Ma. He didn't trust Shipe, but

there was no reason not to listen to what the talkative little Australian had to say. Shipe was a source of information, much of it undoubtedly true, which shouldn't be overlooked.

"It happened once before," said Shipe, his narrow face appearing at the window between the two cells. "Last February. The Chinks took some potshots at a couple of Ivan chemists in one of the rocket labs."

"Why?"

"Be damned if I know. That rocket stuff's too complicated for me. All I know is that the Chinks hate anybody who ain't got slant eyes, an' that includes any Ivans who get too big for their underpants."

Shipe became silent for a moment, and they listened for sounds of more shooting, but heard none.

"Speakin' of rockets," said Shipe. "Did you get a look at that big fish on the other side?"

"I noticed it. What about it?"

"Take another look."

They walked to the south windows of their respective cells and Riley looked half a mile across the base to where two giant gantry cranes were lifting a long missile from its silo. The missile was three-fourths of the way up now, higher than before, and Riley saw that it was an enormous affair of five cylindrical stages topped with a silvery, cone-shaped object which protruded several feet beyond its nose.

"That's the Lenin II," said Shipe. "Biggest Goddamn rocket on the base."

"How come you know so much about it?"

"I keep my ears open," boasted Shipe. "I hear things."

"What's that cone thing on top?"

"That I don't know, Yank. But I been watchin' old Lenin II for weeks, watchin' 'em raise it and lower it, fiddle with this, fiddle with that. And you can bet a shilling on one thing, Yank."

"What?"

"They're going to fire that big fish pretty soon. Any night now. Maybe tonight."

"Do they do all their firing at night?"

"Usually. Speaking of firing, Yank, d'you hear any more rifle fire?"

"No."

Again they fell silent. Riley continued to stare out between the iron bars at the giant missile and he saw that Shipe's statement was correct. The Lenin II was emphatically the largest rocket on the base, at least twice as long and twice as wide as the largest of the others.

Dozens of men swarmed about it, some high on the rigging of the gantry cranes, others at work in and around the concrete silo. It occurred to him that his mission to Takla-Ma could well be linked with the firing of this mechanical colossus. The timing could be coincidental, of course. But it was possible that the radio transmitter in the false stone was to have been delivered to someone on the base who would send back information to McKnight's forces relating to the launching of Lenin II. And if the rocket were going to be launched soon, that would account for Lu's and Fedotov's anxiety and hurry in questioning him. It would explain why they had set up the firing squad so quickly that something had gone wrong.

He felt a sudden burst of anger and frustration. He grasped the bars and tried to shake them, but they did not budge and he felt no relief. It was McKnight's fault. McKnight had good reasons for doing it his way, but if McKnight hadn't been so cautious, if McKnight had only given him more information he wouldn't feel so helpless.

As long as he was still alive, there was always the chance he might escape again. The possibility was remote in the extreme, but *if* he did escape and *if* he did manage to get his hands on the radio transmitter—what the hell could he do about it? He hadn't the slightest idea where to take it or whom to contact.

"Son of a bitch," he said.

"What did you say?" asked Shipe.

"Nothing important," said Riley.

Shipe's face appeared again at their mutual window and he grinned at Riley.

"I say, Yank," he said. "You wouldn't have a crumb or two to drop me, would you?"

"A crumb or two of what?"

"Info, Yank. Just a scrap or two."

"Like what?"

"Like the frequency of that transmitter, for example. Some little scrap like that."

"You bastard," said Riley. "You're no prisoner."

"Sure I am," said Shipe cheerfully. "I'm as bloody well locked up as you are."

"You're a goddamned turncoat."

"Maybe," said Shipe, "but a man's got to live—and to live in this stinkin' place a man's got to be able to trade. Sooner or later, Yank, you'll start tradin' with me. And just to get you in the mood, Yank, I'll offer you a scrap —for free."

"A scrap of nothing?"

"No, fact. I don't mind tellin you, Yank, that you'll be havin' a visitor late this evening—that sweet little piece o' frill named Judith."

"What makes you think so?"

"I *know* so, Yank. And now I'll take a little nap. See you, Yank."

Shipe removed himself from the window and Riley heard the crackling sound of a straw mattress being lain upon.

"Don't forget what I said," Shipe called. "I'll have info to trade whenever you're ready, Yank."

Riley did not comment. He remained at the window, his hands on the bars and stared down thoughtfully at the roof of the building which was under construction near the tower. He thought about the confident things Shipe had said and wondered if it were possible to get the information he needed from Shipe. It would be difficult, because he had nothing to trade in return. Absolutely nothing.

He remained at the window for many minutes, concentrating, watching the work proceed on the giant rocket, occasionally glancing at several Chinese who were laboring on the roof below. The roof was being finished with long, narrow green and yellow tiles.

In numerous places there were collections of stone and sand being used to complete the construction of a parapet which rimmed it. As the afternoon sun slid lower in the sky, the shadows lengthened across the roof and the beige-colored piles of stone grew darker in color. He noticed that one stone, atop a stack midway on the roof, was becoming distinctly a different shade.

As he watched, it occurred to him that McKnight would have equipped the drop capsule with more than one stone replica. The capsule had been nearly four feet long, large enough to contain several replicas which would have landed in several places on the dry marsh. One replica might have been hard to find, but if several had been dropped the task of the finder would have been less difficult.

The stone atop the pile was now definitely more orange than the others. Undoubtedly its color was due to something geological, a formation of quartz and sand which was slightly different from that of its neighbors. It was possible, also, that the stone merely lay at an angle which caused it to reflect more of the setting sun's orange light than the others.

And there was the third possibility.

He knew the chance was extremely unlikely. It was the worst kind of wishful thinking. Besides, if it were one of McKnight's replicas, other parts of the F-121A would have fallen on the roof. He studied the entire tile surface, taking it section by section, but saw no hint of wreckage or stains where wreckage might have lain before being removed. It was possible, of course, that a replica—being light in weight—would not have traveled as far forward as the heavier airplane debris. If that were true, then the replica might have landed on the roof while the wreckage continued to a point further on.

He squinted into the growing twilight, trying to see torn-up or stained areas beyond the building or on the ground beside it. He saw none. And as it grew darker, the stone became the identical color of the others and he became certain his imagination had tricked him into seeing something that couldn't possibly be there.

He heard the door to the adjacent cell being opened and the voices of guards speaking to Shipe in Chinese.

"See you later, Yank," Shipe called. "Have sport with Judith."

The door clanged again.

Riley walked to the window between the cells and looked in. Shipe had departed—no doubt to be quizzed by Fedotov and Lu, who would want to know what he had learned about his prison mate.

In a few minutes Riley's own door was opened by one of the heavy-shouldered Russian guards who now patrolled the corridor as replacements for the Khams. The guard placed two clay bowls on the stone floor and slammed the door shut.

It was the first food and drink Riley had been given since the previous evening. The raisins were hard as pebbles, the rice was unpalatable and the cold tea had been mixed with sour milk curds. Hungrily he downed every bit of it and wished he had more. It was the first time his food had been delivered by someone other than Judith and it convinced him more than ever that Shipe's remarks about her were a lot of loud talk.

But he was wrong.

~⌒(*chapter eleven*)⌒~

She came within a half-hour. She came alone, and after the guard left she stood there with her back to the heavy iron door and did not speak.

She simply stood there, her large brown eyes gazing at Riley with open fear and mistrust.

"My God, Judith," he said. "What's the matter?"

Her hand went first to her cheek, paused and then

89

moved nervously to her mouth. Her white teeth clamped upon her fingers.

"Please," she said. "I—"

Her voice trailed off. She gestured at her hair and clothes.

In the dimming twilight he had not noticed at first that she did not wear her usual nurse's uniform. Stepping closer, he saw that she wore a filmy white Indian sari. It was wrapped skillfully around her waist and breasts, one drape forming a skirt, and the other hanging in a long fold from her shoulder.

There were other things about her which were different. She wore lipstick, a dark red which outlined the full curves of her mouth. There was a circular black caste mark on the lower center of her forehead and her eyelids had been touched lightly with bluish-green eye shadow. Despite the make-up, she still looked scarcely twenty.

"Amazing," he said. "You were lovely enough before, Judith, but now you're beautiful."

His words did not please her. Bowing her head, she covered her face with her palms.

Before she spoke, he knew what she was going to say.

"I am ashamed," she said. Coming from behind her palms, her voice was a muffled whisper.

"You needn't be," he said.

"You have guessed why I am here?"

"Yes."

"You have guessed who sent me? You have guessed who had me dress like this?"

"Yes. And please don't be afraid of me, Judith."

He went to her then, and when he placed his arm across her back she did not draw away. Pulling her closer, he felt her face touch his chest, cautiously at first, then more firmly, and in another moment she was holding on tightly, her arms around him.

She trembled against him, crying without sound, and he felt the warm moisture of her tears dampening his shirt and the skin underneath. He felt a strong desire to

90

caress her and to kiss the side of her neck, but he restrained himself.

After a while she composed herself and looked up at him, rubbing the tears away with her fingertips.

"Do I look terrible?"

"No."

"It is the first time I have tried make-up. Has the eye shadow run?"

"No. But tell me, Judith, did you really think I would take advantage—is that why you were so afraid?"

She nodded.

"Are you still afraid?"

She shook her head. "Not as much."

"Good," he said lightly. "I wouldn't want my woman to feel perfectly safe around me. But you are—temporarily." Lifting her hand, he rubbed it against his day-old growth of beard. "I wouldn't lacerate you with this weed patch, Judith. But if I was shaved—believe me, you'd be in trouble."

She smiled and touched his chin. "They are quite nice. Very mannish."

"Careful," he warned, "When aroused, I'm a tiger."

She drew her hand away, but they remained close together, whispering so the listening devices in the walls could not overhear them.

"Was it Fedotov and Lu?" he said. "Did they send you?"

"Not Fedotov. Lu. Dr. Fedotov is not himself."

"What's happened?"

"He has been drinking since this morning. He is very drunk."

"Because of what happened in the courtyard?"

"Yes. Lu did it deliberately. He arranged it with the Chinese leader of the firing squad while Fedotov was away. The Russian soldiers were not supposed to be killed.

"I didn't think so. Why did Lu do it?"

"Some of the Chinese hate being second to the Russians. I think one of the Chinese generals ordered Lu to do it."

"And now Fedotov is in trouble with his generals?"

"Yes. The Russians have lost face."

"What about the gunfire this afternoon? Did anybody get hurt?"

"I do not know. I do not think so."

"Will there be another firing squad in the morning?"

"I do not know. But I do not think they will try to shoot you—not before the drug is tried."

"The No. 1?"

"Yes. The bad one. Lu insists that it be tried as the only way to make you tell the name of the other agent. The Russians do not want to risk it because if it fails you will never be able to tell them. But Lu is very angry about what happened to him in the courtyard."

"The way Fedotov slapped him?"

"Yes. He has been in a rage all day. He wants very much to be recognized as the wisest of all the Intelligence officers at Takla-Ma. He will take any risk. He will inject you with the No. 1 when he can find it."

"What's happened to it?"

"Dr. Fedotov has hidden it. And this makes Lu very angry. But he is clever and I am afraid he will find it."

"Do you know where it is?"

"No. But I wish so much I did. I would destroy it. It would be horrible—it would be terrifying if it were used upon you."

She shuddered, then bowed her head and gazed at the floor.

"Judith," he said softly, "why are you telling me these things? Do you realize the risks you're taking?"

"Yes."

"Why are you doing it?"

She raised her face. "I am a nurse and all during my training in Kashmir I was told that healing is the finest miracle of man. I believe it is wrong, a crime against God, for man to use medicine to destroy man."

"Very good. But, is there any other reason, Judith?"

"Yes. I hate the Russians. I don't like Dr. Fedotov, but he is better than some of them. He is so very fat and ugly and he tries to touch me sometimes, but he is not like Lu."

"How do you mean?"

She did not answer.

"Judith," he said, "what did Lu do to you?"

She would not look directly at him.

"Please," she said.

"All right, I won't insist, Judith. But if I could get my hands on him I'd break him in half. The son of a bitch. He—"

"Please," she warned. "He will hear you!"

Riley lowered his voice. "All right, Judith. I know there are some things you don't want to talk about. But there's something else I must ask you—and if you don't answer I'll understand."

"What is it?"

"Do you know who the other agent is?"

She remained perfectly motionless for a moment.

"No," she said. "I do not."

He thought of a way to rephrase the question but there was a brief movement of her lashes and an expression of caution in her eyes which told him it would be best not to press the subject.

"I must know something else," he said. "Did you see where the wreckage of my plane came down?"

"Yes."

"Near here?"

"Yes."

"How close to the building that's under construction?"

He tried to keep the eagerness from his voice because he did not want to influence her answer.

"Not too far from it. Part of it came down in a vacant area beyond the building."

"Very good," he said. "I've got to ask you one other question, Judith. I know I shouldn't, but I must."

"Please do. I want to help if I can."

"Could you get a key to my cell door?"

She fell silent.

"I am not sure," she said. "I am not at all certain Lu will let me return here."

"Why not?"

"He threatened me. He told me I must return with information from you tonight. He told me I was to—" She hesitated, her words stopped by her embarrassment. "He said that—" She hesitated again. "He said I must bargain with you. He said that before I offered you what he told me to offer you, that I must get the information from you."

"The name of the other agent?"

"Yes."

"So we're back to that again. Damn it." He brushed his palm hard across his forehead and then rubbed the back of his neck. "Hold everything. I think I've got it. Tell Lu that you learned this from me. Tell him Fedotov knows more about me than he's letting on. Tell him Fedotov won't use the No. 1 drug on me because Fedotov's got some sort of deal cooking with me. You can hint that Fedotov may already know the agent's name and is holding out on Lu. Do you think you can do that?"

"Yes. I think I can."

"Good. Now what about the key? Is there any chance you can get one?"

"Yes. There are many keys in the tower office. I will try to get the right one."

"When will you come back?"

"I will try to come back tomorrow night."

"Can't you make it any sooner?"

"No."

"About what time?"

"Seven."

"Can you bring along some rags—an old dress or something?"

"Yes. What for?"

"For smoke. After you give me the key, go back down the steps inside the tower. Set fire to the rags. Make sure you bring enough for a good blaze. And then pray that there's enough smoke so the guards will leave the corridor and go down to investigate."

"It will be very dangerous," she said. "Do you think

you should try it again—after what happened the first time?"

"Yes, I've got no choice. And I hate to bring you into it, Judith, but you're the only one I can trust."

"I know. And I am glad to be trusted."

"Can I ask you one more question? Are you sure there isn't some other reason behind your willingness to help me?"

"Yes," she said. "There is."

"What is it?"

"Because I think I like you."

It was not the answer he expected. Nor was he prepared for her next movement. Very quickly she raised herself on her toes, pulled his head down and kissed him. It was a swift kiss, but he felt the full soft pressure of her lips and tasted the flower fragrance of her lipstick.

She did not let him embrace her. She went to the door and rapped for the guard.

"That was because you were nice to me," she said. "And because I wanted to."

The guard opened the door and shined a flashlight into the cell. He saw Riley wiping the lipstick from his mouth and he laughed crudely, his meaning clearer than necessary.

"Shut up," said Riley in English. He smothered an urge to smash the guard's head against the sandstone wall.

Still laughing, the guard stepped back and allowed Judith to pass into the corridor.

The door slammed shut.

～❦(chapter twelve)❦～

Dawn came to the Takla-Makan Desert in a brilliant pink haze which sent the violet night sky sliding swiftly before it. Long before the sun appeared, Riley stood at the south window of his cell watching the morning light

95

spread across the waterless dunes in the distance, first illuminating fringes of wind-picked rock which jutted up like prehistoric skeletons, then slowly approaching across the tile roofs of the base's buildings.

He kept his eyes on the largest heap of sandstone on the nearest roof. He watched the light grow stronger, until he could make out the individual shapes of the stones. Soon he saw the top stone clearly.

It was the same beige color as the others. As the sun rose higher, he watched the stone intently, but its color remained the same. He did not permit himself to become disappointed, even though he knew that all his thinking and planning about it could well be a waste of time. There was still the possibility, the longest of long shots, that it might be a replica and that with Judith's help he might be able to deliver it to the other agent.

He remembered the expression of caution in her eyes the night before when he asked if she knew the identity of the other agent. It was possible that she *did* know and that this explained her willingness to help him. She certainly couldn't be blamed for not wishing to risk telling him.

Earlier than usual he heard the sounds of people moving in the corridor. When the cell door was opened, he was surprised to Colonel Fedotov enter. He had expected callers, but not this early, not at five o'clock in the morning.

Fedotov removed his key from the door and put it in his pocket. He did not speak, nor did the uniformed major who accompanied him. As Fedotov came further into the cell, Riley saw that his saffron-colored barracks cap was pushed carelessly to one side of his head, his great round red cheeks were covered with dirty blond whiskers, and the top buttons on his bemedaled tunic were unbuttoned. Around him was the alcoholic odor of vodka. The fumes had the unmistakable sourness of the breath of a man who had been drinking for many hours.

Fedotov bowed in Riley's direction. It was a slight bow, but low enough so his hat slipped off and fell to the floor. The major picked it up and replaced it on Fedotov's head.

Fedotov nodded. He went behind the toilet partition and remained there for a considerable length of time. The major remained with Riley, his expression militarily correct, giving no indication of any thoughts he might have.

When Fedotov reappeared, his hands were at his waist, fastening the front of his trousers across his vast bulging stomach. He sat down on the cot, his weight depressing it dangerously, and his tired, red-edged eyes gazed at Riley.

"Fine toilet," he commented. "Fine Russian toilet."

He rubbed his whiskers and yawned.

"Prisoner Riley," he said, "do you not sometimes wonder why such a valueless person as yourself is stationed in a cell furnished with such excellent plumbing?"

"Yes," said Riley, "I have wondered."

"Yes," said Fedotov. "Of course."

From a pocket in his tunic, Fedotov took some raisins which he placed in his mouth and sucked thoughtfully.

"Five years ago," said Fedotov, "this great missile base was only a prison camp. One of our great Russian scientific leaders fell into temporary disgrace due to a change in government. He was exiled here. Since he was a very important prisoner, his confinement was arranged as comfortably as possible. To impress our Chinese friends, this prison tower was equipped with pipes, a well and a tank of water on top. The toilet was the first ever seen in this entire great region of western China."

Fedotov placed more raisins in his mouth and chewed them. Riley decided that Fedotov was now only partly drunk and had reached a stage where he was mellow and in a reminiscent mood.

"Russian ingenuity." Fedotov tapped his forehead wisely. "When the Americans were in China, they were not clever enough to bring plumbing to this remote area to impress the Chinese. While our great Russian leader, whose name was Lysenko, was confined here, he saw the possibilities of turning this part of the desert, with its reasonable climate, into a great military facility. When he regained favor in Moscow, he recommended that this facility be built. It was a pity that he never lived to see its magnificent completion."

Fedotov shrugged and his eyes became sad. "An airplane accident. No one survived, not even Lysenko." He paused for a moment, as if in tribute, and then continued. "There are many toilets on this base, Prisoner Riley, as many as you have on your bases in America. It is true that sometimes they do not all function. It is true, for example, that the one in my quarters is temporarily—"

"Colonel-Doctor Fedotov," interrupted his aide. "I would like to point out respectfully that your appointment with our marshal will be earlier this morning than usual. I would like to recommend that—"

"Be still!" Fedotov glanced with annoyance at the major. "We shall leave shortly."

He turned back to Riley. "My point is this. Russsia is now the most important military nation in the world, with the greatest missiles and rockets ever devised by the mind of man. We can build anything. Toilets, automobiles, television sets, cigarette machines. And yesterday the United States for the first time acknowledged Russia's greatness publicly to the world."

Fedotov rose from the cot. He drew his bulk up as straight as possible, obviously unaware that the open buttons on his tunic and the awkward angle of his hat made him look like the burlesque of a military figure.

"Listen to me carefully, Prisoner Riley," he said. "Yesterday your President admitted—"

Again Fedotov was interrupted by his aide, more insistently than before it was clear that the major was trying to keep him from saying too much.

"Colonel-Doctor," the aide said, "there is not much time before your appointment with our marshal. I respectfully suggest that—"

"Be still! Be still!" said Fedotov. "There is enough time—and it does not matter what our prisoner hears because he will never repeat it. Prisoner Riley, your President admitted before the world that the United States so fears the power of Russia that it sends spy planes to inspect us. Your President openly admitted the spy mission of the high-altitude U-2 airplane which accompanied you part way on your flight and which was shot down over Russia. This is the first time in history that the leader of a major nation has ever openly made such an admission."

Fedotov paused for breath. "What do you think of this, Prisoner Riley?"

"I have no comment," said Riley. "If the President made such a statement I am sure that he had a good reason. The United States has never been afraid of the truth."

"Of course," said Fedotov. "Of course. But there is an additional significance. At no place in his statement did the President acknowledge the flight of a second spy plane into China at the same time. What do you make of this, Prisoner Riley?"

"I have no comment," said Riley, "but I have a question. Did your government announce the downing of my plane publicly?"

Fedotov smiled so broadly that the heavy flesh of his cheeks became deeply creased. "Very good, Prisoner Riley. Of course not. And I am therefore going to tell you that there can be one reason—and one reason only —for your President's careful omission of mentioning your low-level flight. Of the two missions, yours, Prisoner Riley, was by far the most important. Why? Because of a vital secret on this base which your government is desperate to learn."

Once more Fedotov paused and drew in his breath. And once more he ignored the urgings of his aide.

"I am nearly finished," said Fedotov. "And it is with regret, Prisoner Riley, that I must inform you that the problem you have created for us goes beyond the ethics of medical science. I have advised my superiors against using the *parrie stahreek* injection upon you because its use violates all medical principles and ethics. But now,

99

with your President's own statements emphasizing the importance of these events, I shall be forced to change my decision. That is all, Prisoner Riley. I go now to prepare to meet the marshal."

Fedotov saluted slowly, turned right and marched to the door. Glancing back at Riley, he shrugged, shook his head and went out, followed by his aide.

Riley remained standing for a long interval. Then he sat down on the cot and tried to think it all through. It was possible that Fedotov's statements were merely those of a tired drunken man. But it was more likely that a good deal of it was the truth, and this was supported by the actions of Fedotov's aide.

The aide's nervousness had clearly been that of a man trying to prevent certain things from being said. It followed, therefore, that matters were rapidly drawing to a conclusion. Fedotov and Lu might return later this morning, or in the afternoon, and administer the drug.

He could not remain seated on the cot. He began to walk up and down in front of it. He realized he was pacing and that it was a sign of anxiety and desperation, but he did not stop. His error was too obvious. He should have insisted that Judith come earlier with the key, despite the additional risks.

He heard activity in the adjacent cell, footsteps and the sound of a closing door. In a moment Shipe's narrow, ruddy face appeared at the barred window.

"Mornin', Yank."

Riley nodded.

"Have a nice time?"

Riley did not answer.

"Was I right?" said Shipe cheerfully. "Did the little miss come?"

"Yes."

"You don't sound happy about it, Yank. Something the matter?"

Riley walked over to the southern window and looked down at the roof.

"All right, all right," said Shipe. "Give me the silent treatment. I don't care. But let me hand you a bit o'

100

warnin', Yank. You better tell Colonel Lu what he wants to know."

"Thanks," said Riley. "Now why don't you shut up?"

"Okay, okay. But you better tell Lu—or else you know what."

Shipe laughed and made a gesture of injecting himself with a needle.

Riley turned back to the window.

It went on like that all during the rest of the morning. Shipe talked continually. Riley tried not to let it get on his nerves, but the nasal quality of Shipe's voice was as irritating as cheap chalk scraping a blackboard.

Again and again Riley walked to the southern window and studied the progress of the workmen erecting the stone parapet on the nearby roof below. In the rays of the late morning sun, the stone atop the largest heap of building material was the same color as the others.

From time to time one of the workmen took a stone from the edge of the pile and placed it on the parapet. Riley knew that before long, either today or tomorrow, a workman inevitably would touch the top stone. To keep himself occupied, he tried to guess how many stones were in the heap and how many more would be needed for the parapet, but he soon lost count.

When the cell door opened at noon, he expected Fedotov and Lu to enter. But it was one of the Russian guards with clay bowls of cold curdled tea and a mixture of potatoes and rice.

In the middle of the afternoon, the door was opened again. Riley braced himself. But once more it was the guard, removing the bowls.

From late afternoon on, Riley's trips to the window were more frequent. And now as the sun became lower in the sky, the top stone's color altered slightly. A half-hour later the stone was noticeably more yellow than the others, and by early evening its color was definitely a pale orange.

He saw the workmen pick up their tools and depart and he knew that from this point on everything depended on timing and luck. If Fedotov and Lu came first, the chance for escape would be ended. If Judith came first, there would be a chance, a very small chance, but no matter how small it would have to be tried.

He tried to relax beside the window but he could not. To relieve the tension, he breathed in deeply, and expelled slowly. Although the evening was cool he felt perspiration collecting on his ribs and his palms were moist and slippery.

Time dragged. The sun set and twilight came. He tried not to fidget.

"What's the matter?" said Shipe. "You sick or something?"

"Lunch upset my stomach," said Riley. "What time is it?"

Shipe looked at his wrist watch. "Twenty to seven. Want me to call a guard."

"No," said Riley. "I'm all right."

Estimating the passage of the minutes, he remained beside the window until he thought it was almost seven.

If Judith were coming, she should arrive at any minute.

He walked to the window between the two cells and leaned carefully against the bars.

"Feel my forehead," he told Shipe. "I think I'm running a fever."

Shipe looked at him curiously. He hesitated, then put his hand between the bars and touched Riley's face.

"Good Lord, Yank. You're soaked with sweat. Maybe I better—"

Riley's right hand quickly seized Shipe's wrist. His other hand shot between the bars and closed upon Shipe's throat.

A small forced cry came from Shipe's lips and then he was silent, his milky blue eyes swelling with fright. He scratched at Riley's face. Riley lifted him from the floor and pulled him toward the bars, striking his head against the iron.

It was not difficult to do because Shipe probably weighed less than a hundred and twenty-five pounds. He smashed Shipe's head against the bars a second time and the small man sagged unconsciously, legs and arms loose.

Riley was tempted to drop him to the floor, but reconsidered. It would be easy for Shipe to feign unconsciousness and then scream loudly for help once he was released.

Riley held Shipe against the bars, one hand on his throat, the other grasping his thin upper arm. He lifted Shipe higher until he could see the dial of Shipe's Swiss wrist watch.

It was two minutes after seven.

He heard footsteps coming along the corridor, followed by the sound of a key being inserted in his door. He banged Shipe's head against the bars a third time, harder than before, and let him fall to the floor.

The door opened.

First he saw the greenish-brown cotton trouser leg of a guard. Then he saw someone else.

It was not Judith. It was Fedotov.

Riley did not breathe. He stood rigidly beside the window, his mind turning over haphazardly, trying to determine what had gone wrong. If they had found out about Judith, if they had followed her and trapped her, then it was all over.

Fedotov came in. The guard tried to follow, but Fedotov leaned his great bulk against the door. The guard barely managed to withdraw his leg before it slammed shut.

Fedotov waved one plump hand in the air, smiled at Riley and staggered toward the toilet partition.

"Fine toilet," he said. "Fine . . . Russian toilet!"

Riley's mind began to catch up. Fedotov was alone, unaccompanied by his aides or Lu, a situation which might not continue for long. It was possible that Fedotov might be faking drunkenness to trap Judith. But it seemed more likely that he was really drunk and had wandered up here simply to relieve himself.

"I am uncomfortable," said Fedotov.

Unfastening the belt on his tunic, he went behind the partition.

Again there was activity in the outside corridor. A key turned in the lock and the cell door opened.

This time it was Judith. She came in alone, carrying a tray of food. Her cheeks were pale and as she set the tray down she nervously spilled the tea.

Riley put his finger across his mouth, cautioning her to be silent. He gestured at the toilet partition, indicating someone was behind it.

She understood. Stepping closer, she spoke in a whisper, her lower lip trembling.

"I could not get the key. I tried but—"

"It's all right," he whispered. "Did you get the rags?"

"Yes. I left them on the steps. But you must not try it. It is impossible. There are many men in the tower, extra guards—"

Abruptly Fedotov spoke from behind the partition. "Someone is there? Colonel Lu?"

Riley put his lips close to her ear. "For God's sake, don't argue!" He pushed her toward the door. "Light the rags and get down from the tower as quick as you can. Hurry!"

She rapped on the door and the guard unlocked it. As she went out, she glanced back at Riley and her large brown eyes glistened with uncertainty and fear.

The lock clicked as the guard shut the door.

Riley stepped to the partition doorway and looked in. Fedotov sat with his trousers down, his elbows comfortably resting on his fat pink knees, his round face supported by his hands. He was gazing at a chestnut-colored cockroach which lay on its back on the floor, its legs working helplessly.

As Riley came in, Fedotov looked up. The movement of his head lifted his fat chin to exactly the right place for Riley's first blow. He struck the chin as hard as he could and it was like crashing his knuckles against a pudding. The soft flesh slowed the force of the blow only slightly. Fedotov's head snapped back and his arms flew up. His skull cracked against the porcelain toilet top.

It should have been enough. But it wasn't. Fedotov

seized Reiley's arm. Either from shock or fear, his grasp was fantastically strong. He pulled himself partly upright, his enormous weight forcing Riley to bend forward. Riley drew his right arm back and struck again. This time he did not aim at the cushiony chins. He struck Fedotov on the bony forehead projection directly above his eyes. The blow seemed to have no effect. He drew his fist as far back as he could and struck again, in the same place.

Fedotov collapsed all at once. His great weight began to slide off the toilet. Riley grasped his shoulder and tried to prevent it, but Fedotov's bulk was entirely too much. The tunic slipped through Riley's fingers, ripping off medals and ribbons. Fedotov landed on his side, wedged between the white porcelain and the wall, head twisted, his plump lips flattened grotesquely against the yellow sandstone.

Riley went swiftly through Fedotov's tunic pockets and as many of his trousers' pockets as he could reach. He did not find the key.

From the corridor came the sounds of running feet and shouts and he hoped they meant Judith had lighted the rags successfully. Grasping Fedotov's fleshy right leg, he exerted all his power and finally managed to budge him. Then by successive jerks he moved the unconscious form across the floor and part way into the outer cell.

In Fedotov's rear pocket, he found the key, a large brass affair decorated with Chinese characters.

As he straightened up, a voice began to shout into the cell, coming with abrupt fury.

"Guards!" the voice shrilled. "Guards!"

Turning, he saw Shipe clinging to the window bars, blood pouring from cuts on his head, his mouth wide open, screaming as loudly as he could.

⚛ chapter thirteen ⚛

Riley did not bother with Shipe. Shoving the key into the lock, he opened the door and ran into the corridor.

He saw no guards. From the stairway entrance, twenty feet away, came a thin, twisting streamer of black smoke. It was not nearly as much as he'd hoped for.

"Stop him!" screamed Shipe. "Guards! Guards!"

Riley ran to the stairway entrance and looked down into the darkness. He saw more smoke, a great deal of it, plus a few sparks, coming up from two landings below. He heard the voices of several guards cursing, and the sounds of boots stamping out flames.

Riley ran up the stone steps which led to the roof of the tower. He expected to find a locked door, but there was none, and when he reached the flat, tile roof he saw why a door was not considered necessary. From up here, the tower seemed extremely high, far too high for the leap he planned. It was only one story higher than his cell, but this meant his leap to the roof of the adjoining building would be four stories. He realized he had miscalculated. He had planned on a jump of three stories.

From below came Shipe's voice, gaining strength and shrill volume.

"Guards! Guards! Stop him!"

For ten seconds, twenty, Riley remained motionless, staring through the darkening twilight at the roof below, estimating the distances. The tower was twenty feet from the courtyard wall and the roof of the other building was another four or five feet beyond. This meant his leap would have to cover at least twenty-four or twenty-five feet horizontally as well as the four stories vertically.

He had never leaped more than twenty-three and a half feet in the broad jump during his best days at UCLA. And that had been ten years ago.

"Guards!" screamed Shipe. "Guards!"

And now there were other shouts below and the sounds of guards' boots on the stone steps.

Riley ran past the water tank to the farthermost edge of the tower's roof. He turned around, crouched slightly and began his sprint.

He ran át top speed across the roof, traveling about ten yards before he reached his take-off point. He kicked off with his strong right foot.

At first it was no different from the leaps at UCLA. He arched upward and out, as in a conventional broad jump, the wind swishing past his ears. But then he began to drop, following a slanted path, and now he sensed the difference. Desperately he whirled his arms to keep his body balance up. The sound of the wind increased against his ears, hissing like a jet's slipstream at Mach 2.

The drop went on and on. Until the last second he wasn't sure he would clear the stone parapet. His heels missed it by inches and he landed in the construction sand a few feet beyond. The impact was three times as bad as he expected, the sand hitting him like hard cement. Pain flashed up his legs and along his spine. Instantly he fell forward onto his face and stomach, exploding the air from his lungs, rolling over and over helplessly until he crashed into a pile of sandstone.

He didn't know whether he was unconscious for a time, or whether he simply lost track of what had happened. He found himself hobbling in a half-crouch along the roof, both his legs and his spine burning with pain. His left leg was by far the worst, so crippled it dragged and gave him little support.

The twilight seemed darker than when he'd started his leap and he wondered if he had injured his vision some way. Halting, he stared about, trying to get his bearings, trying to find the largest of the piles of sandstone.

Everything looked different than it had from above, too gray, too third-dimensional. He heard men's shouts coming from the tower, but they seemed unreal, too far away to be true. He hobbled to the pile of stones, but in the darkness he could not determine which was the top stone.

He lifted several but they were too heavy. He saw another which was about two feet long, seemingly too large, but as soon as he touched it he knew. It was much lighter in weight than the others and its surface had the molded smoothness of plastic. He placed it under his arm and hobbled on, looking for a way to get down from the roof.

He felt no exhilaration, no thrill of accomplishment. Instead, seeing searchlights flashing from the tower and hearing more shouted commands, he knew that disaster and failure were nearer than ever.

He had to find Judith and quickly. Without her help, he couldn't possibly make it. He had achieved something in finding the replica, but if he didn't deliver it to the right person, and soon, this failure would be more miserable, more bitter than his first escape attempt.

Stumbling over unseen stones, he cursed with frustration and anger. He could see no stairway leading down from the roof and although he was only two stories up he could not risk another leap, not with his leg aching so badly.

When the top of a wooden ladder rose ghostlike in the gloom ahead of him, he turned away quickly, ready to leap and to hell with the consequences. But a voice restrained him. Judith's voice.

"This way! Hurry!"

He saw her climbing higher on the ladder, beckoning to him.

For a moment he gazed at her stupidly, unable to comprehend where she had come from.

"You're hurt," she said. "Can you get down?"

Her words, taut and urgent, brought him out of it. He went toward her and saw that she had placed the ladder up into an unfinished skylight opening in the roof. Holding the stone replica tightly under his arm, he followed her down the ladder's worn crossbars to the dark interior of a large room which was cluttered with construction material.

"Hurry!" Judith said. "There is no time."

Her small hand took his firmly and she led him past sawhorses and scattered lumber into a dark hallway. They walked for many minutes, passing numerous dark doorways, traveling so far that Riley thought the hallway might have no end. At last she led him down a stairway to what appeared to be a nearly completed anteroom. She gazed through a window into the street beyond.

"This is the worst part," she said.

She waited. Then she pulled him toward a door.

"Now," she said. "Hurry!"

His left leg gave him hell, fighting every step as they ran across the street into a large sandstone building on the opposite side. From somewhere nearby came the sound of sirens and gunfire. They went up concrete steps and into the warm and brightly lighted hall of an apartment building.

"Hurry!" said Judith when he stumbled. "Oh, my God, hurry!"

They rushed along the corridor, passing wooden benches and occasional yellow clay vases filled with shabby artificial flowers. Riley smelled cooking odors, cabbage and potatoes, and knew they could not continue on much further without encountering someone.

Judith halted before a rough wooden door. As soon as she tapped, it was opened by a middle-aged woman who admitted them swiftly into a small kitchen and shut the door.

Riley recognized the woman at once. She was the administrator with the mannish haircut who had made an inspection visit to his cell along with numerous other Takla-Ma officials two days previously. She was a thin woman of perhaps fifty, wearing a drab brown skirt and a man's white shirt. Her face was pale and drawn, but her dark eyes were intensely animated.

"Praise our Lord!" She spoke in English and made the sign of the cross upon the breast of her shirt. "Did anyone follow you here?"

"Not that I know of," said Judith. "I—"

"Be silent," said the woman. "I will listen."

She placed her cheek and ear against the wooden door, remaining there motionlessly for half a minute. Then, satisfied, she turned and looked at Riley and Judith.

"It is good," she said. "No footsteps. At least I do not—"

Abruptly she gave a small cry of excitement.

"What is this?" She stared at the object beneath Riley's arm. "How can this be?"

She tried to touch the stone replica, but Riley turned and prevented her.

"It is all right," said Judith. "She is Madame Lysenko. She helped plan your escape."

"Lysenko?" said Riley. "The designer of Takla-Ma? Are you his wife?"

"His widow," said the woman. "And your collaborator. Please, may I see the object. It is extremely vital."

Riley nodded. "In a moment, Madame. But first you must prove certain things to me. I'm sure you understand."

"Of course." She hesitated, as if refreshing her memory, and then spoke several phrases rapidly, pronouncing the words in a crisp, efficient English. "Mercury Beach. Astronauts. You were the eleventh ranked candidate in the program. Your former serial number was 0330360. The records will show that this information was not touched upon when you were questioned under the drugs of Fedotov and Lu. Their records also will not show·that during my trips to Western Europe I have worked with your General McKnight directly and indirectly since last year. Is that sufficient identification, Major?"

"Enough for now." Riley grinned at her with relief and handed her the stone replica.

She placed it on a rough but clean wooden table. With her thumbnail, she operated a small fastener and the plastic replica separated into two oval halves, revealing the gleaming metal parts and red, green and blue wires of a transistor radio transmitter.

"Thank God!" she said. Then, mystified, she gazed at Riley. "But this is not the one found found by Fedotov and Lu. How did you obtain this?"

"Luck," said Riley.

"More than luck," said Judith. "He was magnificent. He leaped from the tower and located it on the roof."

"The Lord is good to us," said Madame Lysenko. "Perhaps he will continue to be good."

Again she made the sign of the cross. Then she went to her knees and bowed her head. Her pale lips moved in the words of a prayer.

Rising, she turned to Riley and spoke respectfully and apologetically. "I am sorry, Major, that I could not contact you more directly at the tower and do more to help you escape. I have long been ashamed of the tactics of such men as Lu and Fedotov and many other leaders here at Takla-Ma, but I have been forced to keep my feelings secret, for reasons which must be clear to you. Even Judith, bless her, has not known the true nature of my work. For a person untrained in espionage she has done well, has she not?"

"Very well," said Riley. "Without her help, I couldn't possibly have made it from the tower."

Abruptly there were the sounds of voices and soldiers' boots in the hall outside the door. Madame Lysenko raised a cautioning finger to her lips, then gathered up the sections of the transmitter.

"Into the other room," she said. "Quickly. The soldiers may come here and search."

They went into a bedroom. Madame Lysenko drew aside a thin blue cotton drape on the opposite wall, revealing a door which opened into another room not much larger than a walk-in closet.

"Major Riley," she said. "You will remain hidden here. At least for tonight."

She turned to Judith. "And you must return to the hospital. At once—before you are missed."

"No," said Judith. "I cannot."

"You must. You know what will happen?"

111

"Yes, but I cannot. And it is not just because one of the guards saw me disposing of the flask of kerosene after I started the fire."

"Where did he see you?" Riley spoke calmly, concealing his anxiety. "In the tower stairway?"

"Yes. He noticed me near the first-floor sentry office when I dropped the flask into a trash box. He and the others were too concerned then with the smoke and fire to stop me. But that is not the main reason I cannot go back." Judith tried to prevent her mouth from trembling, but did not succeed. "I cannot face Lu again. I cannot."

"She's right," said Riley. "She can't go back. By now the guard will have reported her and they must be hunting for her as carefully as they are for me. She'll have to stay here."

"Yes, of course," said Madame Lysenko. "There is no going back now—for any of us."

Her dark eyes were somber for a moment, revealing how fully she was aware of the way their difficulties and perils would mount in the coming hours.

She handed the transmitter sections to Riley. "Keep these with you. I am sure I need not say it, Major, but you must protect these with your life. Do you know what the radio will be used for?"

"I can guess," he said. "To send out information concerning Lenin II?"

"Yes. It will be fired within twenty-four hours, possibly sooner. Now quickly inside with both of you."

She closed the door behind them, and Riley heard her draw the outside curtain in place. Examining the small room, he saw that it was about eleven feet long and four feet wide. It was dark and windowless, with light provided by a flashlight on a shelf, and poor ventilation provided by a small hole high up in the sandstone wall. The room's furnishings were restricted to a three-legged wooden stool and a narrow bed made of wood and canvas.

Riley sat down on the bed and rubbed the calf muscle of his left leg.

"Is it better?" Judith asked. She remained beside the door.

"Much better. Only a sprain."

Her large brown eyes studied him uncertainly. "Perhaps I should—" Her voice trailed off and then she began again. "Perhaps I should stay in the other room where I—"

"Of course not." He made a place beside him on the bed and then he spoke gently. "Sit down, Judith. You have nothing to be afraid of. Surely you know me well enough by now."

"I am not afraid," she said. "I wanted to come here. I wanted to be alone with you, in this small room, if only for a little while. But—"

"But what?"

Bowing her head, she refused to look at him. The light from the flashlight was reflected softly by the strands of her thick black hair.

"What is it, Judith? There's something you've wanted to tell me. Can't you tell me now?"

"No. I cannot."

"I think you should try, Judith. I think you must."

"Yes," she said. "Perhaps."

She raised her head and looked at him. Her eyes were filled with pain and shame.

"I am not what you think I am," she said.

He felt a strong desire to help her, to say something comforting, but he did not speak.

"I am not a good person," she said. "I am not virginal."

She covered her face with her small hands and wept.

∽✦(chapter fourteen)✦∽

He let her cry for a few moments, then he went to her. He lifted her into his arms and carried her to the bed. He placed her gently upon the canvas and then he knelt

113

beside her, stroking her sleek dark hair. Before long she was breathing more quietly, weeping only a little, lying there with her eyes closed.

"Now you must tell me," he said. "All of it."

"Yes," she said.

"And you must keep your eyes closed so I can—"

He kissed first her left eyelid, and then the right one, touching his lips softly to the warm smooth skin, feeling the silky touch of her lashes. Then he folded her small hands into his.

"Now," he said. "Begin."

"Yes. From the beginning." She was silent for a moment and then she spoke in low, subdued tones. "It began about two years ago in Srinagar, my home in Kashmir. Srinagar is a very old city, an ancient beautiful city dating back to the third century before Christ. But the old ways have been changing. For many years they have been changing. My mother long ago gave up the old religion and became a Christian. And when she married she did not choose an Indian man. My father was an Englishman from Birmingham and they had three daughters. I was the second daughter and like all good Anglo-Indian girls I loved my parents very much."

"In that we're alike," said Riley. "I'm from a mixed marriage also. My mother was Mexican, my father American."

"We are lucky," she said. "I think stronger people come from mixed marriages. It was two years ago that a great new freedom for women swept across India. Women were no longer forced into the old ways. We walked the streets as proudly as men and dressed as we liked.

"Some of the girls, not used to this freedom, went too far. They wore gauzy saris and flimsy trousers and low-cut cholis which revealed too much of their bosoms. I did not do this. Instead I fell in love with a student at the hospital where I was in training. Like my mother before me I did not choose an Indian. He was a Russian medical student and when he asked me to go away with him to Stalingrad I went gladly."

She opened her eyes, but Riley kissed them shut.

"Keep them closed."

"Yes." She drew in her breath sharply. "His name was Anton. He did not love me. He did not marry me. And so I was made to discover in that difficult way that I did not love him either. I wanted so much to go home, back to beautiful Srinagar. But I had no money and I was too foolishly proud to write my mother and father and ask for some.

"When the Russians asked for volunteer nurses for work in China, I came to Takla-Ma without knowing what kind of a place it was. I came because I thought I would be closer to India. Working for Colonel-Doctor Fedotov was not good, but fortunately he was too fat. But Colonel Lu terrified me from the beginning. And one night when I was on late duty at the hospital, he—"

She turned her face away. She breathed more rapidly, her body so tense that the small tendons stood out in her throat.

"Tell it," said Riley.

"I cannot! I cannot! I have never told anyone, not even Madame Lysenko! I—"

"Tell it! My God, Judith, surely you must realize that you are not the only woman ever to be assaulted. Tell it!"

"Yes!" she cried. "He did that to me. He took me into one of the unused rooms. He tore my uniform. He tore my underclothes. He put his unclean body upon me. And now I am unclean. And I shall always be!"

Gently he turned her head and kissed her throat, keeping his lips there until the tendons relaxed and then he kissed her mouth.

"You're wrong," he said. "Don't you see how wrong you are about yourself, Judith? He stole from you. You had nothing to do with it. You are the same person you were before it happened. He changed nothing."

"But there is more," she said. "There is Anton. He pleaded with me. He begged me. And finally I—"

"You gave in?"

"Yes."

115

"How many times, Judith?"

"One time. Only that once in Stalingrad. And it was no good. It was no good from the beginning and I—"

"That's enough, Judith. There is no reason for you to remember more." He kissed her mouth again. "And now I want you to open your eyes."

But she did not open them.

"Look at me, Judith. I want you to look at me while I tell you something very important."

Slowly her eyes opened.

"I think you know what I'm going to say," he said. "I think you must know that it is different when two people are really in love. And isn't that why you came here, Judith, to this small room with me? You knew, didn't you, how I felt about you?"

She did not speak. But her eyes did not leave his face.

"Didn't you, Judith?"

She nodded. "I hoped so. So very much, I hoped so."

"I have known many women," he said. "Many, Judith, but I could never say these words to any of them. I love you, Judith. Not because of what you've done, and you have done a great deal for me. I love you because of what you are. A perfect person."

She rose up on the narrow bed and placed her hands on the sides of his neck.

"I thank God," she said. "I thank God very much."

She put her mouth against his and held him tightly, pressing herself against him.

"I believe it," she said. "It must be different when a man and a woman are truly in love. It must be then as God intended it to be. And I know now, deep inside, that this is why I came here. Because I wanted, because I needed—"

She removed her hands from his neck. She slipped off her shoes. Then she lay back down on the narrow canvas bed and slowly unfastened the small button at the collar of her white uniform. Her large brown eyes looked up at him, shining softly in the subdued yellow rays of the flashlight.

He bent over her. He had no wish to hurry. He un-

116

fastened the second button, the third one, and all the others from her bodice to the hem of her uniform.

Gently he helped her arms from the sleeves and then he removed her cotton slip, her white bra and the white briefs. She was lovely, the lines of her body slim and firm. Leaning down again, he placed his lips in the darker division between her pale ivory breasts. The skin was extremely warm and as she drew in her breath her breasts rose beautifully and touched his face. Their contact filled him with a sudden drive of desire, a spreading force that demanded possession of her at once but he did not heed it.

He did not allow himself to hurry. He slipped from his clothes and then he went to her, placing himself on the bed. As soon as he touched her, she cried out and her legs became unyielding, resisting him.

"Judith," he said softly, "listen to me. You are the loveliest I have ever seen. And to me you are very, very virginal."

She came to him then, her body relaxing against him, giving him sweetness and fire, sensation and beauty beyond anything he had ever dreamed of knowing. She looked up at him, loving him, proud of him and proud of herself. She smiled then and closed her eyes. He touched her breasts with both palms, stroked them and felt them grow tense, felt the beautiful desire growing within her. He let his hands remain there, felt her flesh rising and falling more rapidly. Then he kissed her deeply on the mouth.

At once she came even more beautifully alive. Alive with love for him. And they knew they were sharing something remarkable. This was excitement and desire far beyond body and flesh. Because, more than excitement and desire, it was love. And it was as though it had never happened like this anywhere in the world before.

They lay close together afterward and he placed his chin against the soft abundant strands of hair at the top of her head. To keep off the chill of the night, she wore her uniform dress, partially buttoned with nothing beneath it. He was shirtless, and through the thin cotton of his trousers he could feel the warmth of her body as if there were no clothing between them.

"Now I know you were right," she said. "It is so different if you are in love. So very different. Was it for you, also?"

"Yes, Judith. Far, far different. I have never—"

The sound of gunfire interrupted him, coming from outside the building, but not too far away, perhaps less than a hundred yards away. It was a machine gun, firing a quick dozen shots, becoming silent and then releasing another burst of sound. Judith trembled violently and he stroked her arm and shoulder, calming her.

"What will we do?" she said. "Where will we go?"

"I don't know."

"Can we leave Takla-Ma?"

"Maybe. If the fighting grows worse."

"It will be dangerous, won't it?"

"Yes, Judith."

"But you will take me with you?"

"Of course."

The machine gun was no longer firing. A man shouted loudly in Chinese, and then ran close beside the building, his boots making strong vibrations as he passed.

The night became silent again.

"Now it's my turn to talk," he said, "and I want you to listen carefully, Judith, and make a judgment for yourself."

"You need not."

"But I will. Because you are entitled to know. And because if we ever leave here, it will affect whatever we might be together."

"Then tell me," she said.

He spared her none of it. He told her everything about his night on the beach with Fay Exler, the wine, the swimming, the lusting and the blow that broke her neck.

When he finished, Judith did not speak immediately. Then she raised her lips and kissed his forehead.

"I have sympathy for her," she said. "But I have more sympathy for you, knowing what you have felt since,

118

how hard it has been to carry those thoughts about her within you. You did not have to tell me, but I love you more because you did."

He drew her close once more and touched his lips to her eyelids, her small nose and her mouth.

"There's more," he said. "Something else to tell you, but it can wait."

"Yes," she said. "Let it wait. And let us be silent now and think thoughts of luck for one another. And in the morning I will show you what I have thought."

He felt drowsy. "You say funny things, Judith, but they're nice."

"Be silent," she said. "Sleep. In the morning I will show you our luck."

He closed his eyes. And although he heard the sound of the machine gun again, farther away now, he slept.

⌒◁(chapter fifteen)▷⌒

A monstrous roaring and a rumbling of the earth awakened him. For a moment he did not stir because he knew what it was. They were test-firing the engines on the great Lenin II and their roar was an assault on the eardrums—tremendous sound that made more than the bed shake and tremble. It vibrated the sandstone wall beside the bed, the ceiling and set the flashlight to dancing on its wooden shelf. It lasted for only a few seconds, ten at most, and then the sound ended quickly, as if cut off with the slash of a giant blade.

Opening his eyes, he discovered that Judith was no longer on the bed beside him. The flashlight had grown dimmer, but there was enough light to show him that she had left the small room.

He sat up. In a moment there was a tapping on the door and Madame Lysenko spoke.

"Major Riley? Judith? Are you up?"

119

Coming more fully awake, he realized something was wrong. He put on his shirt and opened the door.

"Good morning," said Madame Lysenko. "It is early, only six o'clock, but I thought we should make our plans."

"Where's Judith?" he said.

"Judith?" The woman's dark eyes grew puzzled. "Is she not with you?"

"No."

"Are you quite certain?"

Stepping to the doorway, Madame Lysenko looked into the small room.

Riley seized her thin shoulder roughly and turned her around.

"Where is she? What did you do with her?"

"I have done nothing." Madame Lysenko seemed mystified and uneasy. "Perhaps she is—"

Riley brushed past her. He glanced around the bedroom, noticing the unmade bed where Madame Lysenko had slept and a door that led outside. He strode into the small kitchen, saw that everything was in order and returned to the bedroom.

"Why should she leave?" he said angrily. "What made her do this?"

He did not wait for Madame Lysenko's reply.

"Where does this go?" he demanded, approaching the outside door.

"To the side street. But do not go out. There are soldiers everywhere, looking for you. Takla-Ma is being turned upside down. Some of the Chinese are in a rage, fighting the Russians, blaming them for your escape."

"Were you here all the time?"

"Calm yourself," she said. "She will return."

"Answer me! Were you here all the time?"

"No, I was not. I was gone for thirty minutes to my office in the Administration Building, where I received reports on the Lenin II. The launching is tonight, and with the final countdown to commence at seven-thirty."

"To hell with the launching! I've got to find her. Before she's picked up."

He went to the door, but Madame Lysenko moved more quickly. She pulled his hand from the unpainted wooden doorknob and then placed her back against the door, preventing him from opening it.

"Have you lost your mind?" Her dark eyes flashed at him. "They will arrest you seconds after you leave here! They will see where you came from and you will destroy everything I have labored for, everything General McKnight has labored for—and everything you yourself have labored for!"

He wanted to strike her down, dislodge her from the door and take his chances outside. But he knew she was right. He stood there a moment more, staring at her, still feeling the anger and fear, and then he turned away.

"You are wise," Madame Lysenko said. "Come and have a cup of tea. Judith will return. Soon, I am sure."

He sat on a hard wooden chair in the kitchen and drank the hot spicy brew too quickly, burning his lips and tongue.

When he was on his second cup, and still drinking too rapidly, there was a light tapping on the bedroom door.

"It is she!" said Madame Lysenko.

She opened the door and Judith came in swiftly, out of breath, her brown eyes sparkling with a curious happiness. Riley put his arms around her, embracing her tightly, placing his cheek against hers which was cool from the outside morning air.

"You little idiot!" he said. "Where did you go?"

"I told you," she said. "But you were too sleepy to listen."

"Told me what?"

"About our luck. Our wonderful luck. And here it is."

She drew back a step. From the side pocket in her white uniform dress, she carefully lifted a piece of paper which had been formed into a cup. Inside the cup was a handful of damp sandy earth. Growing from it was a small plant with two shiny green leaves.

"A silver birch!" she said happily. "Our ancient tree of luck. I have tended it for many days there beside the hospital."

"You went after this?" He tried not to sound too incredulous. "Did anyone see you?"

"Yes. A few soldiers. But it was dark, very dark, and I do not think they got a clear look at my face. They asked me where I was going and I told them I was about to go on duty in the main ward. So they walked with me a short distance. There are other nurses in the ward and I was fortunate none of them recognized me."

"They walked with you?" Riley seized her shoulders, holding her so tightly she winced. "My God, Judith, don't you realize the risks you took? What happened after that? Did they follow you? Do they know where you went?"

"I do not think so. But I cannot lie to you." She lowered her eyes. "Later they noticed me again, when I was leaving the hospital grounds. One of them must have seen me clearly because he spoke to the others and they all ran after me. But I ran faster and they could not catch me. And then I—"

"Then you came here?" said Riley.

She nodded, glancing first at him and then at Madame Lysenko, biting her lower lip when she saw how concerned they were.

"Think carefully," said Riley. "Were you followed anywhere near this building?"

"No," said Judith. "I do not think so."

"How many soldiers did you see?" asked Madame Lysenko. "Do not be afraid to tell us, Judith. Is the area swarming with soldiers?"

Again Judith lowered her eyes. "Yes. Many of them."

"Hunting for Major Riley and yourself?"

"Yes. I am sorry I did not think about the danger to us all. I thought only about the little tree." Judith held the plant close to her face and breathed its fragrance. Then her dark eyes glanced up softly at Riley. "Can you understand the importance of this little tree?"

"Not exactly."

"It is our miracle," she said. "A seed like this growing in the dry desert. I know you think I was foolish, but we must have it with us. In my family a silver birch has

122

always brought good fortune. And this little tree will be our good fortune. Do you understand now?"

"I guess so." He drew her closer, so glad to have her back he did not want to press the matter further and destroy the happiness and security which the small tree seemed to have brought her.

"You are angry with me?" she said. "Be truthful."

"Yes. A little bit."

"It will pass." Judith rubbed her face lovingly against his shoulder. "And I will not leave you again. Ever."

"Enough!" interrupted Madame Lysenko sharply. "Back into the room, both of you. It is growing very light and they will soon be searching every corner of this building."

"Can you keep them out?" said Riley.

"The soldiers, yes. The corporals and sergeants, yes. They must respect my rank as administrator. But later, perhaps this afternoon, the officers will come and then it will be a different matter. They will want to know what is behind the curtain. Now get inside. Hurry."

She held the door open for them. As they passed her, a sound came from the kitchen, the abrupt authoritative rapping of knuckles on the corridor door.

"You see." She made the sign of the cross. "Hurry!"

She closed the door and Riley heard the curtain being drawn back into place, followed by the sound of her footsteps leaving.

He and Judith stood behind the door, listening. For a minute they heard nothing, and then Madame Lysenko returned, drawing the curtain and opening the door.

"Soldiers," she said. "Looking for you, Major Riley. When they saw who I was they did not ask to be admitted. But they will make a report to their next-in-command."

Entering the small room, she picked up the two sections of the radio transmitter and placed them side by side on the wall's broadest shelf. She untied the halves by plugging in several of their wires and then opened up a slender telescoped aerial which extended eight feet, almost to the ceiling.

"It is well to be ready," she said. "When the time comes to send the signal, there will be very little warning."

"A few seconds at most," said Riley. "Where will your signal be picked up?"

"In Turkey."

"By a U.S. listening post?"

"Yes."

"And you realize what else will happen as soon as you touch your sending key?"

"Yes."

Madame Lysenko shrugged her thin shoulders. It was a simple shrug, but it told better than words that she had carefully considered all the possibilities before making her decision.

"I do not understand," said Judith. "What will happen?"

"The Russians will hear her signal at the same time," said Riley. "Within minutes, they will learn where the signal is coming from and will rush here and arrest her."

Judith's small hand sped to her mouth, but not in time to conceal her gasp.

"Do not be afraid, Judith," said Madame Lysenko. "By then you and he will have left here."

"But you?" Judith stepped closer, touching Madame Lysenko's arm and gazing at her pale, tired face. "What will happen to you?"

"It will not matter," said Madame Lysenko. "I will have done what I must do."

"Why are you so willing?" said Riley. "Because of your husband?"

"Yes." Madame Lysenko pressed her dry lips together firmly. "I do not wish to boast, but he was perhaps the finest missile scientist in Russia. He did not want his probes used for war, but for the exploration of space. He was too strong-minded for his own good, spoke out to openly, and that was why he was first imprisoned here, at Takla-Ma. Later when they needed him he was removed from disgrace and began the work that was his life's dream—the designing of the great Lenin II. When the designs were finished, he learned that the great rocket would not be used for space exploration as he had dreamed, but would be used instead for war research."

"Atomic?" asked Riley.

"Yes. The Lenin II contains Russia's first C-bomb. It is the cobalt bomb, a device more fearsome and terrible than the H-bomb. Our Russian leaders are aware that America has had the C-bomb for several years, but has not tested it because of the international agreements recently reached at Geneva banning atomic tests.

"Our Russian leaders plan to test their C-bomb secretly, sending it as much as fifty million miles into space where its detonation will be analyzed and the information used for making more C-bombs. My husband opposed those plans with all his energy. So they destroyed him. And, godless people that they are, they were willing to destroy fourteen other men who were with him on the flight."

Madame Lysenko moved her hand slowly through the air in the fluttering gesture of a falling plane.

"That was four years ago," she said. "I still weep about it, when I am alone where no one can see me. Our Russian leaders do not know that I learned about the sabotage of the airplane, and they do not know that this compelled me to do my best to press on with my husband's work. They are not sensitive enough to know what can live for years in a woman's heart.

"My husband and I did not have children, though we prayed to God many times to be blessed. So our love was wholly for each other and we were drawn closer together by our scientific work. When he was killed, it was the end of my life also. So, you see, what happens to me after tonight will have no real significance."

Madame Lysenko ran her fingers over the top of her close-cut gray hair. It was the first sign of nervousness she had displayed.

"We must succeed," she said. "We *must!* And I am sorry, Major Riley and Judith, but I will need you here to help me until the last minutes."

"You'd have to dynamite to get me to leave," said

Riley. "By staying here I've got a chance to prove to McKnight that he sent the right boy on the job after all. What information will you radio out?"

"Two statistics. The exact second when the Lenin II lifts off the ground, plus the fact that its warhead will be detonated 1,021.11 hours after lift-off. As administrator of the calculating division, one of my duties is to co-ordinate such data. Our calculating machines did not determine the detonation hour until this morning, which is why I visited my office. When America receives these statistics, she will send a rocket into space almost simultaneously and as far."

Madame Lysenko smiled at Riley. "I can see by your face that you did not know America has a rocket as powerful as Lenin II. But this is true. Your rocket probe will travel into the same area of space and analyze the C-bomb data. Perhaps America will then decide to test its own C-bomb. I do not know, because that had not been decided six months ago when I met briefly with your General McKnight in Austria.

"But I do know this. When I could no longer stomach how my husband's designs were being perverted and misused, I took my first furlough from here to Russia and thence to Vienna. My mission for the Russian government was the purchase of scientific supplies for Takla-Ma, but I also had an assignment from my own conscience. It was difficult for me to make the initial contact because it went against many of my old habits of thinking."

"You must have thought about it a long time," said Riley.

"Yes. But once I spoke to a representative of the American Embassy I knew I had done the proper thing. And on my next trip—when I met your General McKnight and set up our plans for your flight—then I knew for certain that my course was clear and just. General McKnight agreed with my husband's philosophy. He agreed that the important thing is for each nation to be equally strong, with the same atomic potential. So long as each nation has information on the other's terrifying strength, we will have peace. A stalemated peace, yes. My husband knew this was the best which could be achieved now. But it was his prayer that someday the nations of the world would be united in a truly lasting peace in their mutual need to explore space."

Madame Lysenko touched the radio transmitter affectionately, making a minor adjustment on its wiring. "Now you know, Major Riley, why I was so overwhelmed last night when you came here with this. I had given up all hope and it was almost impossible to bear." She stepped into the doorway and smiled almost gaily. "Now, my fine young people, what would you like for breakfast? Sausage and potatoes, perhaps?"

"Let me help," said Judith. "May I peel the potatoes?"

"No thank you." Madame Lysenko shook her head wisely. "Stay here with your major. Learn more about him and see if he would make a good spouse. I shall enjoy cooking for you both today. It has been a long time since I cooked for anyone other than myself."

While Madame Lysenko worked in the kitchen, Riley shaved with a straight Swedish steel razor which had belonged to her husband, standing before a small mirror held up by Judith. Madame Lysenko brought three plates into the small room, setting them on the cot, and they began to eat.

Before they were halfway through, someone rapped on the kitchen door. It was a quiet knock at first but it became quicker and more urgent.

Madame Lysenko closed the door and drew the curtain. In a minute Riley and Judith, standing behind the door, heard a man's voice coming from the kitchen. Another minute passed. Footsteps came into the bedroom and now the voices were clearly distinguishable.

"You're welcome to look," said Madame Lysenko.

"It is a formality," said the man.

Riley recognized the voice. And he knew by the way Judith suddenly trembled and grasped his arm that she recognized it also.

It was Colonel Lu's voice, sardonic and very self-confident.

"The soldiers saw her," he said. "They thought she came to this building. I respect your rank very highly, Madame Lysenko, and it is with the deepest respect that I come here. And what is this?"

Riley heard the curtain being jerked along its rod.

"And this?" said Lu sarcastically. "Is this a door, Madame Lysenko?"

"Yes. The door to another apartment."

"And why do you keep it covered?"

"It is never used. And it is unsightly."

"I see," Lu paused. "Then you will not object if I open it?"

Riley pushed Judith away from the door and he prayed that Lu did not hear the frightened intake of her breath.

He concealed himself beside the wall, close to the door. The doorknob turned and Riley braced his legs and raised his hands shoulders high.

The door opened a few inches and stopped. The toe of Lu's dusty black boot came into the opening and nudged the door carefully back.

Before it was completely open, Riley sprang. There was no time to decide the proper moves. He leaped at Lu's throat, grasped it with both hands and then saw, too late, that Lu was bringing a black pistol up into aiming position. His rush carried Lu backward into the bedroom. Riley knew he had to do something about the pistol, but he did not want to risk losing his grip on Lu's throat. He got his knee behind Lu's legs, toppled him and twisted his body so that when they fell Lu's pistol arm was trapped beneath his hip.

Lu was muscular and quick. As they struck the floor, he rolled, trying to throw Riley off and at the same time freeing his pistol arm.

The black barrel came up again, trying to aim at Riley's chest. Riley's left hand shot away from Lu's throat, caught his wrist and bent it back until the dark eye of the muzzle aimed upward. Instantly he felt the oily skin of Lu's throat slipping away from his other hand.

Riley started to shout at Madame Lysenko, but it

wasn't necessary. Darting toward their outstretched hands, she pulled the pistol from Lu's grasp and retreated.

A burst of wet air came from Lu's lips, but Riley shut it off by clamping both of his large hands around the man's throat, sinking his thumbs into the soft area just below the Adam's apple.

No matter what Lu did, no matter how he kicked, clawed or twisted his body, Riley did not ease the deep pressure of his thumbs. It was a long time before the last of the strength left Lu's legs, and a longer time before his sharp-nailed yellow brown fingers relaxed, stiffened, and then relaxed again.

At last Riley rose. So great had been his concentration that he had not realized Judith was clinging almost hysterically to Madame Lysenko, her face turned away from Lu, her breath coming in long, racking gasps. When Riley touched her, Judith seized him violently, and it was many minutes before she became calm enough to look up at him and speak.

"I could not—" Carefully she kept her eyes away from the unmoving figure on the floor. "I could not help it. Seeing him again. Seeing the gun and knowing what he would do to you—"

He brushed back a wisp of dark hair which had fallen across her temple and then touched his lips to her forehead.

"It's over," he said. "Part of it, at least, Judith. And even if nothing else goes right, at least we'll have the satisfaction of knowing the son of a bitch will never touch you again."

She shivered as if chilled and held him more tightly.

⌐⌐(chapter sixteen)⌐⌐

In the early evening, with the launching forty-five minutes away, Madame Lysenko returned from her final visit to the Administration Building. Hurrying into the small room, she walked erectly, cheeks flushed, dark eyes alert and tense.

"How did it go?" said Riley.

"Very difficult," she said. "All is disorder."

"What about Lu? Is he missed?"

"Yes. The search for him is nearly as great as that for you and Judith. The inquiring about him is reaching to all levels of authority. I was questioned myself, quite closely."

"Did they doubt you?"

"I do not think so." Madame Lysenko gestured helplessly. "But it was impossible to be sure. Everything is so upset, so badly disorganized."

"What about the fighting?"

"It is much worse. But it will not affect the launching. The Chinese are flexing their muscles, showing their anger and their superiority of numbers, but they are eager to see Lenin II fired exactly at seven-thirty and will not attack the launch area. Nor will it be necessary. Chinese technicians are in control of the blockhouse and will fire Lenin II on schedule. Meanwhile, Chinese soldiers have captured three companies of Russian troops on the far western side of Takla-Ma and are beginning a drive to take over the entire base."

"Can they succeed?"

"Yes. This is not skirmishing as before. The Russian leaders did not realize this soon enough. To please the Chinese commanders, our Russian marshal sentenced Colonel Fedotov to death for inefficiency, but the action came too late. By tomorrow the Chinese will overwhelm us. They have used your escape and the disappearance of Lu as angry excuses, but those are not the real reasons for the fighting.

"The Chinese have long resented the Russian use of Chinese territory for missile experiments. But more than that, they resent our technological successes. After they capture the base, the Chinese will claim the launching of the great Lenin II as their work, their success, and will demand recognition in the world as a major atomic

130

power. Do you realize the significance of this, Major Riley?"

"My God, yes. Red China will be a fantastic atomic threat. So it's more important than ever that the U.S. know about Lenin II's launching and get its own C-bomb tested in space."

Madame Lysenko nodded soberly. She removed her gray administrator's smock and placed it on a shelf near the radio transmitter.

"We must not fail," she said. "We *will* not fail."

"What happens later? Will the Russians bring in more troops and try to recapture Takla-Ma?"

"No. That would mean all-out war, which Russia does not want."

"Did you check the catapult site?"

"Yes. It does not look good."

"What's wrong?" For Judith's benefit, Riley tried to keep his words from sounding tense and stiff. "Is the jet still there?"

"Yes. And so are a dozen men. They are trying to repair the catapult which was damaged by a Chinese grenade."

Riley cursed quietly. "What about the next site? How far is it?"

"Far. A mile, possibly more."

"Did you inspect it?"

"No. I could not take the time." Madame Lysenko shook her head slowly. "I wish there was some other way. It bothers my conscience that I was the one who brought Judith into this, seeking her out at the hospital, using her to contact you. During these terrible days, I have grown to love her like a daughter and the thought of the catapult, the danger of going there—"

"Forget it," said Riley, more sharply than he intended. "We have no choice."

"I am ashamed of you two," said Judith cheerfully. "Have you forgotten our luck? Have you forgotten our tree?"

"It will take more than that," said Madame Lysenko.

"To keep you safe will require all our prayers and the strong will of God."

"What time is it?" said Riley.

"Forty minutes to countdown." Madame Lysenko turned and went toward the kitchen. "I will prepare the food and then we will take up our stations."

"I'm not hungry," said Riley.

"Nor am I," said Judith.

"Later you will be," said Madame Lysenko. "This food is to take with you."

Smiling at them, she worked skillfully at the counter of the large wooden cupboard, slicing dark bread, making enough thick sausage sandwiches for several men. Only once did she stop smiling. That was when she stooped and opened the lower cupboard drawer, revealing a small portion of Lu's doubled-up legs. She drew out a gray napkin, wrapped the sandwiches in it, and was smiling again when she returned to the small room. It was a tense smile, forced up at the corners, but it was good for morale and Riley was grateful for her effort.

"How much longer?" he asked.

"Twenty-five and a half minutes," she said. "My watch is co-ordinated with the firing panel in the blockhouse."

"Good. Let's get started."

He sent Judith to the bedroom's outside door and told her to report the sounds of any voices or approaching footsteps. Then, while Madame Lysenko turned on the transmitter's switches, he took her binoculars and climbed partway up the sandstone wall, supporting his feet on the wooden shelves. The room's ventilation hole was only six by four inches, too small to accommodate both lenses of the binoculars. One lens was enough, however, to give him a view of the Lenin II.

The great missile was a mile, perhaps a mile and a quarter, away. Because of the obstructing roof of a nearby building, he could not see all of it. But he saw the important part, the top third of the rocket, with its silvery, cone-shaped warhead silhouetted against the deep twilight blue of the sky. The missile stood alone now, its two towering gantry cranes many yards away on either side.

"It's ready," he said.

"Excellent," said Madame Lysenko. "Twenty-three minutes."

He kept his eye against the lens. Far to the left of the Lenin II, the radar antenna of a tall telemetering tower began to swing back and forth, nervously studying the sky.

"Twenty-one minutes," said Madame Lysenko.

As the final countdown approached, Riley expected the time to drag, but instead the minutes began to speed and he felt perspiration on his forehead and around his eye, slightly fogging the binocular lens. He heard Madame Lysenko speaking softly to herself in Russian and knew by the measured rise and fall of the words that she was praying.

"Eight minutes," said Madame Lysenko suddenly.

"Seven."

"Six."

And then, swiftly, the final minute arrived and he felt the heavy, rapid beating of the blood in his throat.

He heard her counting off the last seconds, her voice steady but extremely tense.

"Now!" she exclaimed.

And at the same instant Riley felt the building begin to shake and the binoculars eyepiece vibrated against his brow. A swift second afterward the roaring sound came and it was as if a hundred great waterfalls had combined to blot out all the other sounds of the world. He saw the sky light up as if the sun had suddenly appeared, and saw a narrow object, the final umbilical cord linking the missile with earth, drop away from its upper flank.

Slowly the silvery warhead began to rise.

"Lift-off!" he shouted and he wondered if Madame Lysenko could hear him.

And now vast clouds of pure white steam were exploding into the sky, but the silvery warhead rose more swiftly. The higher it climbed, the greater the sound became and a high-pitched, screaming, sirening noise accompanied the rumbling and roaring. Riley's eardrums began to ache.

"It's away!" he shouted.

He lowered the binoculars because they were no longer needed. The tower of yellow white flame went straight into the sky, dropping brilliant liquid sparks, and in a few seconds it was beyond the limited view of the ventilation hole.

He leaped down from the wall. He saw Judith standing in the doorway, her hands pressed tight against her ears. Madame Lysenko leaned close to the transmitter, her face lined with concentration, her hand operating the sending key, repeating the code signals.

When the motions of her fingers paused, he put his face close to hers, shouting against the tremendous sound of the rocket.

"Contact?"

"Yes!" She nodded eagerly. "They have it!"

She sent the signal again. Raising her other hand, she gestured toward the doorway.

"Go!" she said. "Judith and you must go!"

Judith ran to Madame Lysenko and kissed her on the lips. The older woman embraced her and then pushed her toward the doorway.

"Go! Before the soldiers come!"

Riley took Lu's pistol from the shelf and pushed it into his trouser pocket. Judith followed him to the bedroom door and they stepped outside.

High overhead the rocket flame was still brilliantly visible, arcing now as it went south. They walked along the narrow street in the shadows beside the apartment building. Abruptly Judith halted and grasped his elbow.

"Must we?" Her face was white and stricken as she looked up at him. "Must we leave her there? Must she face them alone?"

"She knows what she's doing," he said. "She wants it that way."

He took Judith's arm and hurried along the street. As the rocket's noise dissipated, finally disappearing, the other sounds of the base returned. From the west came the blasts of grenades and mortars and the busy sound of a machine gun. On a street a block away a convoy of a dozen Russian trucks rattled past. Headlights extinguished, loaded with soldiers, they were rolling toward the fighting area.

Judith chose a route along remote side streets and between buildings under construction. They crossed a long, dark parade ground, passed under a barbed-wire fence and approached a small stone building which reeked with an odor familiar to Riley's nostrils. Jet fuel. From nearby came the noise of heavy hammers and the grunts of workmen.

Leaving Judith beside the building, Riley went forward until he could see what the men were doing. They were working in the darkness without lights. There were more than a dozen Russian soldiers at the site, half of them swinging hammers, trying to straighten the catapult's badly damaged steel rails. Nearby was more evidence of sabotage. The wooden supports of the steam tank had been blasted, toppling it over. It had fallen close to the long fuselage of a MIG-25 perched on a truck trailer.

Riley returned to Judith. "No go," he said quietly. "Too much damage."

They walked back to the parade ground and then turned east to a section of the base which Riley had not seen before. In the darkness they lost their way, and an hour passed before they approached the second catapult site. It was dark and silent. Its wreckage included a MIG-25 which had been blown into a huge, torn-metal flower by a grenade placed in its cockpit.

"Can you find another site?" Riley did not succeed in keeping his disappointment hidden.

Judith shook her head. "What can we do now?"

"Go back. It's lousy but it's our only hope."

Blocked by a new truck movement of troops along their route, they chose a different way back toward the first catapult site. They entered a shallow dry gully which slowed their steps because its surface consisted of soft sand studded with rocks and stones. After ten minutes of rough going, Riley was ready to chance another detour, hoping for a better path. But as they climbed the gully's scaly slope, they heard someone approaching from above.

Riley shoved Judith down beside him and they lay huddled together on the incline. The sounds of boots came closer. Raising his head, Riley saw the shadows of two men moving along the irregular rim of the gully. Armed with rifles slung on their shoulders, they appeared to be Russian soldiers on patrol. Both men halted, looked down into the gulch and then walked on.

But in a moment they halted again. One of them made a comment and came part of the way down the slope. Riley moved his right hand slowly to his trousers' pocket and withdrew the pistol. Despite his caution, the barrel made contact with something in the darkness, dislodging a walnut-sized rock or lump of earth. The object made no noticeable sound during the first portion of its tumble down the slope, but created an audible thump when it struck the bottom.

Immediately the two soldiers plunged down the slope. The first man failed to see Riley and Judith, but the second one did and shouted a warning to his companion. Riley could have fired then, with a good chance of downing them both, but he could not risk the chance that the shots would bring others to investigate. As the two men unslung their rifles, he ran toward them.

He put a good shoulder block into the midriff of the first man and bowled him over into the second man. All three of them tumbled down the slope in a tangle of knees, ankles and elbows.

Riley held on to the pistol. He landed hard on his side in the rocks. One of the Russians got to his feet first and swung his rifle at Riley's head. Riley dodged, but the soldier was skillful, corrected his swing and the wooden stock crashed against Riley's neck, knocking him onto his back.

The soldier moved the rifle to his shoulder and his eyes glinted as he aimed at Riley's chest. Riley kicked with both feet as powerfully as he could and sank his heels into the softer flesh of the man's upper thighs. The soldier tried to step backward, missed his footing on the rocks and fell.

He rose, trying to aim the rifle again, but he didn't make it. Riley made a short, swift stroke with the pistol and felt the butt's solid contact with the man's cheekbone. He struck again, hitting jawbone and the man bellyflopped against the rocks and was still.

Riley turned quickly, ready to take on the other man, and was astonished to see him lying unmoving on his back, one hand touching a pen-sized cylinder which projected from his chest.

Judith knelt beside the man and she did not speak as Riley moved closer. He saw that the pen-sized cylinder was the dark wooden handle of a small kitchen knife which had gone into the man's heart.

"I had to!" said Judith, her voice taut and breathless. "He was trying to get up! He would have shot you in the back!"

Abruptly she began to wail like a child in great pain. The sound of her own voice seemed to stimulate her hysteria and before Riley could get to her she released a piercing shriek. He pressed his palm across her mouth and forced her to lie down in the sand, crouching close over her face, using his upper body to muffle the sounds she made. She struggled against him, breathing violently through her nostrils, her shoulders quivering.

"Judith!" he commanded. "Listen to me!"

But for a long time she did not heed him, kicking uncontrollably, trying to twist her body out from under him. Finally sheer lack of oxygen weakened her and she struggled less. He slid his palm partly away and let her breathe through her mouth.

"Listen to me, Judith," he said. "You *had* to. Don't you understand? You *had* to!"

She nodded weakly and he saw that she was coming out of it.

"You were amazing," he said. "Where did you get the knife?"

"Madame Lysenko. It's her—"

137

She shuddered and he was afraid the hysteria was starting again, but she set her lips stiffly and fought it off. "Her sandwich knife. Madame Lysenko gave me her sandwich knife to take along and I—"

"That's enough," he said. "Don't talk about it. Do you think you can move around now?"

"I think so."

They climbed the slope of the gully. The truck convoy had gone on, and they were able to return to their original route. In half an hour they again approached the first catapult site. They moved more slowly and warily than before. They lay close together behind a thick hummock of sand and listened to the sounds of the workmen's hammers.

The moon, full and unnecessarily bright, rose in the cloudless eastern sky. Soon afterward a small sedan arrived at the site. It was the same kind of model used by Fedotov's and Lu's intelligence aides and Riley watched uncomfortably as two men got out and spoke to the working soldiers, gesturing to the west.

A six-wheeled truck arrived. The soldiers dropped hammers, clambered aboard, and the truck drove away, followed by the small sedan.

Riley stared at the site, unable to believe that its sudden silence and inactivity could be real. He allowed a minute to pass and then, gambling that they were alone, he pulled Judith to her feet and they ran to the long, low truck trailer which supported the MIG-25.

"Can we go?" she said. "Is the catapult repaired?"

"No." He lifted her first to the metal trailer and then to the aluminum wing. "We're going to take a hell of a chance."

The canopy was open and he helped her down into the cockpit. The MIG-25 was a large fighter with afterburner and extra fuel tanks, and there was space for her behind the pilot's seat-ejection mechanism.

"Do not look so worried." She smiled confidently as she fitted herself into the cramped hollow. "See. We still have our luck."

Reaching into her pocket, she drew out the bent paper

138

cup and lifted the tiny tree triumphantly into the moonlight.

"You idiot," he said. "You wonderful idiot."

He jumped down to the trailer and went to the large power box bolted to its forward end. Its electric cables were on spools which unwound easily as he carried the plug-in ends to the access door on the jet engine's port side. He fastened the plugs tightly, returned to the power box and switched on its batteries.

Leaning into the cockpit, he lost time hunting for the start-stop switch, which was located on the main instrument panel instead of on the right forward console where he'd expected to find it. He pressed it, the starter spun hard and as soon as he got 6 r.p.m., he opened the throttle to idle. She ignited with a loud blast from the tailpipe, and he knew the noise would carry for a mile, alerting a major section of the base.

He dropped back onto the trailer, unplugged the cables and locked the engine access door. Returning to the cockpit, he strapped himself in and donned the metal helmet the Russian pilot had left hanging on the center pedestal. He reached back, found Judith's hands and showed her how to grasp his straps.

"Hang on!" he said.

He shoved the throttle forward and back, increasing power and decreasing it, forcing the airplane to jerk and rock. He repeated the process until the wheels jumped over their wooden chocks. The airplane rolled heavily down the ramp off the trailer, bounced over the catapult wreckage and then turned suddenly as the right wheel wedged against something. He increased power and the wheel became free. The left wing brushed hard against the fallen steam tank as he made the tight turn away from the catapult area toward the parade ground.

He braked to a quick halt and closed the clear plastic canopy. He shoved the throttle all the way forward, got 100 per cent r.p.m., and released the brakes. The airplane leaped ahead as if swatted, rolled thirty or forty feet and its ten tons of moving weight tore through the barbed-wire fence as if it were straw.

Off to the left, running figures appeared. Russian soldiers with rifles. More than a platoon of them, and they opened fire at once. Riley touched the nose wheel button, turned the airplane slightly left and tripped a rocket release switch. Three of the long, slim cylinders departed from under the left wing, creating three distinct fiery trails. The rockets swept within a few yards of the soldiers, scattering them, forcing them to fall to the ground. The trails sped five hundred yards further to the mess hall and detonated in a tower of flames and spinning stones.

Riley switched on the bright wing lights. He pulled the afterburner handle, adding the thrust of several thousand additional horsepower. The airplane rolled across the parade ground at sixty knots, eighty, one hundred.

Too soon the wing lights revealed the rapid approach of the parade ground's boundary and he knew he did not have sufficient speed for take-off. He brought the stick back and the airplane lifted off slightly, enough to clear a ditch at the end of the parade ground. The wheels touched down again on a rough dirt road beyond. The road led straight toward a cluster of two-story stone buildings. At most it was four blocks long, still not enough running room for an airplane as heavy as this one.

Even when the headlights of a truck convoy appeared in front of the buildings, he kept her fastened to the road. He made her stay down until the last possible second and then he moved the stick back to his stomach.

She came up quickly and beautifully. He hit the wheel retraction lever and seconds later glimpsed startled Russian faces behind a truck windshield a few feet below the starboard wing.

She went up better than he expected. She cleared the roofs by a dozen comfortable feet and went on up cleanly without staggering or vibrating. He let her hang on her nose, climbing almost straight up until the altimeter read five hundred kilometers, and then he leveled off because he wanted speed.

In less than a minute Takla-Ma was a diminishing twinkle of lights miles behind.

He looked back to see if other MIG-25s were rising from catapults, but, thanks to the effective sabotage of the angry Chinese, there were none.

He touched Judith's hand and knew by the warm answering pressure of her fingers that she was all right.

He went out at top speed the way he had come in, flying low to frustrate their radar, zigzagging, and welcoming the full moon as a friend. It lighted the floor of the desert, marking the rock ridges and the dunes, telling him when to climb, letting him know when it was safe to go low again.

For the next hour he flew in a state of numb exhilaration, certain they would make it, but still finding it very hard to believe. When he saw the mountains of India, he broke radio silence, calling a Twelve-Twelve monitoring station, identifying himself in code and asking permission to land at the first available air strip.

"Permission granted," radioed a brisk American voice. "Will clear Koramka strip for landing. Will send jet escort. Will you wiggle wings for identification."

"Will wiggle," said Riley, grinning against the radio mouthpiece.

Removing the helmet, he placed it on his lap, and turned sideways so he could smile at Judith. He lifted her up partly from her cramped position and put his lips against the soft skin near her ear.

"Thank God for your tree," he said.

"*Our* tree," she said happily.

"Ours," he agreed. "Do you know where we're heading?"

"No."

"Northern India. Near your home."

For a moment her eyes were pleased and then, vanishing like a shadow, the happiness was suddenly gone from them.

"Will you leave me there?" she said.

"Of course not. Have you heard of Florida?"

141

"Oh, yes!" The happiness was back in her eyes. "Many times!"

"Have you heard of Mercury Beach?"

"No. Is it beautiful?"

"As beautiful as Srinagar. And we'll find a place to plant your lucky tree."

"*Our* lucky tree."

"Yes, Judith, our tree."

He touched his lips to her forehead, and then he turned and drew on the helmet.

Ahead, glistening in the moonlight, the green hills of India rushed closer.

THE END